BOTTLE RABBIT AND FRIENDS

ff

BOTTLE RABBIT AND FRIENDS

Bernard McCabe

*illustrated by
Axel Scheffler*

faber and faber
LONDON · BOSTON

First published in 1989
by Faber and Faber Limited
3 Queen Square London WC1N 3AU

Photoset by Parker Typesetting Service Leicester
Printed in Great Britain by
Richard Clay Ltd Bungay Suffolk

A CIP record for this book is available from the British Library
ISBN 0-571-15318-6

For Jane

Contents

Bottle Rabbit and the Boxers

One summer's day, the Bottle Rabbit and Emily, that startlingly beautiful white cat, were out for a stroll. They pottered along as they liked to, Emily picking a few buttercups and daisies, the Bottle Rabbit just brushing his woolly paws through the wild goldenrod and meadowsweet. He loved the feel and smell of it, and Emily rather liked the way the yellow pollen clung to his black paws. By and by they came across something quite strange.

'Bottle Rabbit,' said Emily, 'what's that kind of round white stone thing in the ground?'

'I don't know, Emily, but it's got a big iron ring sticking up in the middle of it.'

'You know what? I think we should give it a pull and see if it moves.'

'Looks heavy.'

'Yes, but let's try.'

'All right.'

'Better not stand on the stone.'

'What? Oh, I see what you mean.' The Bottle Rabbit got off the stone. 'Look,' he said, 'I'll lean over and pull with one paw; you pull hard on my other paw.'

'Good idea.'

So the rabbit braced his woolly body and pulled as hard as he could on the iron ring. The whole

thing came up very easily, and the two animals peered interestedly down into a deep hole.

'Look, Emily, it's got steps.'

He was right. All the way down, turning and turning and turning, were neatly carved white steps, clean as ivory, turning and turning so far down that they could not see the bottom, though there seemed to be a pale light down there.

'What do you think?'

'It's a long way down.'

'Let's give it a try, anyway.'

So Emily and the Bottle Rabbit started climbing down the turning stairway. It was interesting all the way down, because the walls were all covered with bright paintings – of sheep, of laughing dogs and smiling buffaloes, some leaping about, others playing chess and cards. At the very bottom they looked back up and saw the white steps curling

2

up and up, and at the top they could see the sky like a little tent of blue shining high above them.

'Now what?'

'Well, there's that big door,' said Emily.

'I'll give it a push,' said the Bottle Rabbit.

Heavy though it looked, it swung open quite easily, so they both poked their noses round it.

What they now saw was a long silvery room with windows almost down to the ground, a polished oak floor, rich carpets and sofas in painted colours, and long low tables bearing hothouse flowers and dishes carelessly displayed with dates, figs and a very large number of arrowroot biscuits.

'Do you think it's private?' asked the Bottle Rabbit in a low voice.

'Well, yes, but look at all those signs.' Over a big davenport were many fretworked notices:

Vilkommen!
Welcome!
Soyez le bienvenu!
Make Yourself at Home!
Feel Free to Avail Yourself of Our Amenities!
All Refreshments Gratis!

'Gratis means free,' said Emily. So the two animals walked in and sat on a sofa. It is true that Emily hesitated just a moment as she heard the heavy oaken door thud shut behind her. She looked round, and kept looking round. She had a funny feeling, though she could not say why. So she said nothing.

Now the Bottle Rabbit loved his arrowroot

3

biscuits. (And they are not all that easy to come by these days.) So he advanced a careful paw and took a couple. He was making himself comfortable on the sofa and nibbling into the first one with his sharp front teeth when a sudden hard loud arrogant voice said,

'Got you!'

'Sorry?' said the Bottle Rabbit, sitting bolt upright.

'Got you! I said got you. Caught you red-handed, by Jove. Nobody wolfs my arrowroot biscuits and gets away with it scot-free, you sam. Got you!'

The Bottle Rabbit wanted to protest. He began to motion with a half-bitten biscuit to the signs saying 'feel free to avail yourselves' and 'refreshments gratis'. Also he was definitely not wolfing his biscuit, simply nibbling. Also his name was not Sam. But the voice had been so harsh and unfriendly that his whole body went cold. He couldn't munch another munch on his arrowroot biscuit, one of his absolute favourite things to eat.

Emily also was very disturbed.

'What was that, Bottle Rabbit –?' she began.

'Don't *talk*. *Shut up*. I don't want to hear a lot of *talk*. Just sit there. Don't worry, we'll be in for you in a minute,' bellowed the Voice.

The animals were appalled. They had never heard anything like this before in their lives, and didn't know what to do, especially as they couldn't see the person who was speaking, or rather baying. There was just a Voice, coming through some sort of loudspeaker. It was worse still when half-a-dozen brutal-looking Boxer dogs came swaggering into the silvery room and looked them over in a sneering way. They were lean and hungry-looking, with shining leather skins and bloodshot eyes. They didn't really come close,

they just slouched about and drooled, and breathed on them. Emily and the Bottle Rabbit tried to keep calm as the heavy dogs moved round them.

'Come, you,' grunted the biggest dog.

The two meekly stood up and followed him. The other Boxers crowded in round them, and hustled them through the second door and down a bare corridor to what looked like an iron-barred cage, or prison cell. Keys clanked, a metal door slammed shut, and they were locked in. All the ugly animals scrambled away.

'Who was it? What was it?' gasped the Bottle Rabbit.

'What was what?'

'That – that Voice that shouted at us so horribly.'

5

'I didn't see,' said Emily. 'I didn't see any face or anything. Yes, it did sound horrible.'

'No more horrible than *you* sound, both of you,' the Voice came booming at them in the cell. 'I don't know who *you* are, the white one, but *you* there, Rabbit. Yes, you. Now listen, Rabbit. First, I want that Bottle. And I want it *now*. Give it to the big dog.'

'But it's *mine*. It's my magic Bottle,' cried the Bottle Rabbit, outraged.

'That's why *I want it*, fathead.'

'Well, I'm not going to give it to you. It's mine. It's my own private property.'

'Suit yourself. You like roast beef and Yorkshire pudding, I expect? With plenty of gravy? Not to mention arrowroot biscuits? Well, I'll tell you now, there'll be nothing to eat tonight, *or* tomorrow, for you *or* your friend, if I don't get that Bottle. See how you like that,' boomed the loud hard Voice. There came a long outburst of overbearing laughter, and then there was silence.

'That room with the arrowroot biscuits and nice smell was a trap,' whispered the Bottle Rabbit.

'Speak up. I can't hear you,' bellowed the Voice. He probably did not realize it, but he had given away an important point. Emily grasped at it.

'Well, that's one good thing. At least we can whisper,' whispered Emily. 'Listen, Bottle Rabbit, give him the Bottle.' The rabbit made a horrified gesture. 'No, don't worry yourself. I've got a sort of plan. Say "Oh all right, take the confounded Bottle then."'

'Oh all right, take the compounded, I mean,

6

take the confounded Bottle then,' shouted the Bottle Rabbit in a trembling voice. He was terribly upset. With shaking fingers he took it from his pocket and laid it between the bars of the cage.

Immediately the door to the corridor opened and the pack of Boxers came thumping down the corridor towards them once again, their little bloodshot eyes glittering, their flabby jowls shaking, their brindled snouts twisted in smirks. The big dog grabbed the Bottle.

'Oh do be careful with it, it's the only one,' the Bottle Rabbit could not help shouting. Emily squeezed his paw reassuringly.

The big dog just snarled, 'See you,' and the Boxers all shambled off, snorting and yapping and grinning, and slammed the door behind them.

For a while nothing happened, but soon the Bottle Rabbit and Emily heard some angry shouts and then much heavy barking and growling from the long silvery room.

'They'll never be able to get it to work, you know, unkind animals as they are,' whispered the Bottle Rabbit, 'but Emily, you mentioned a plan?'

'Yes, listen –' she began, but at that moment the door at the end of the corridor burst open once more, and the pack of Boxers came loping down yet again, with scowls on their wrinkled muzzles. The big dog, who had hardly spoken up to this point, now bared his teeth and said,

'Boss he say him Bottle no worky, him Bottle belong you no worky, Boss he say Bottle no worky you no chop chop.'

The poor animals stared at one another.

'What does *that* mean?' asked the Bottle Rabbit.

7

'I'm not sure, but I think he's saying if the Bottle doesn't work we won't get anything to eat.'

'Well, I'm pretty hungry,' said the Bottle Rabbit.

The big dog growled and grunted and paced up and down. Then he said, 'Boss say he go couchy-couchy, Boss say he try Bottle come sunup, he say Bottle no worky you no marmalade no baconegg no arrowroot, Boss say Bottle no worky we plenty bite you.'

At this all the Boxers burst into roars of nasty laughter and capered about and snapped at one another with enormous teeth and bright red gums. The Bottle Rabbit, who knew exactly why his Magic Bottle was not working (for one thing he'd got it as a Kindness Prize in the first place, and it would only ever work for very kind people), looked indignant and was going to speak. But Emily placed a delicately restraining white paw on his furious black paw.

'Very well,' she said calmly to the big Boxer, 'tell your, er, Boss, that we shall explain it all to him in the morning.'

'You better, missee; Boss he come topside baimbai belong all times *ausgezeichnet* motorbike come bottomsides jug jug all out rain stopped play.'

'What's all *that* mean then?' said the Bottle Rabbit.

'I don't know,' said Emily, 'I really don't know.'

The Boxers moved off, laughing and joking among themselves, arrogantly splaying their feet about and bunching their muscular shoulders. Their sterns jogged stiffly up and down and their stumpy docked tails waggled. One or two of them looked back at the two sad animals and said something disobliging to the others. More bursts of laughter. The Boxers certainly looked fierce and threatening, but there was also something clownish about them.

'Silly billies,' said the Bottle Rabbit, blinking hard, as the door slammed shut again.

Now Emily was moving about behind him. He turned round to ask her again about her plan – she was stretching and bending and twirling her tail.

'Emily, what *are* you doing?'

'This is part of my plan. Don't you see?' she whispered. 'The Boss has gone to bed (at least I assume that's what that barbarous creature means by couchy-couchy), and with a little careful catwork I can now slip through the bars of our cage and find a way into the long silvery room where I am convinced they have left the Bottle.'

'Wonderful, Emily.' The Bottle Rabbit danced about in his excitement, his paws thudding on the floor of their cage. Then he stopped and clasped those paws together.

'But Emily, how are you going to get into that room if the door's locked?'

'Don't worry, Bottle Rabbit. Cats have ways. Cats know.'

The rabbit brightened. 'That's true, of course. But do be careful, Emily. And, oh, by the way, if you *are* in there, I don't suppose you could put your paw on just a couple of – '

'Arrowroot biscuits, *I* know. Well, I'll see what I can do.' Emily smiled and slipped out between the bars, something that the plump Bottle Rabbit could never have managed. She padded silently down the corridor and tried the door at the end.

9

Locked, of course. But Emily, with one of those wonderfully adroit quick bounds that only cats are capable of, was up on a high little windowsill before the Bottle Rabbit could blink twice. He saw the end of her charming white tail give a little wave, and then she was gone.

Time passed slowly. It must now have been deep in the middle of the night. Everything seemed so silent and odd and murky to the lonely rabbit as he paced up and down the cage all alone. Somewhere a fox screeched. He thought he saw an old toad go hop-hopping down the corridor, but it didn't answer when he called to it. He wished it would say something, anything. He was very hungry now, and sad thoughts crowded into him.

'Oh, how happy we were, the two of us, Emily

10

and me, in the woods among the buttercups and meadowsweet and then again on those lovely white steps, coming down and looking at those beautiful paintings,' he thought. 'What demon was it that made us step into that dark backward and abysm, the arrowroot-biscuit room? Oh, how often one thoughtless step can change well-being into misery!' And other things like that.

For a time the Bottle Rabbit was lost in such darknesses. But a slight sound changed all. A quiet key turned, the door in the corridor swung open, and there stood his brilliant white cat friend, smiling away, with a huge bunch of keys and two arrowroot biscuits in one paw, in the other – the Magic Bottle. Outside, dawn was breaking.

She had the cell-door open in a trice and the Bottle Rabbit leapt out, munching away. The two friends ran lightly down the corridor and back into the silvery room where Emily slammed and locked the door behind them. There was now only the heavy door between them and freedom. They stared happily at each other as the Bottle Rabbit reached for yet another arrowroot biscuit. But their agony was not yet to be over.

'*Put* my arrowroot biscuit *down*. The *impudence*! What are you two *doing* out there? You should both be *crouched* in your cell.' It was the horrible Voice again, woken up. It spoke some more:

'*Get* them, Hannibal. *Shove* 'em back in. And no need to be gentle when you do it.'

A ferocious clamour of barking and howling broke out somewhere close by. Then there was a slithering and cracking of sharp-nailed dog-paws. Soon something heavy crashed against the door

Emily had just locked. Clearly she and the Bottle Rabbit now had to get out fast.

She was trying key after key on the heavy oaken door that would lead them to their liberty, while crash after crash came against the other door. One raucous dog-voice, certainly Hannibal's, yelled high and fast above the others: 'Boss he say bite 'em good, Boss he say bite 'em proper. Hah, bite rabbit bite cat.' Now there came a terrible scratching and heaving. The thinner wood on the inner door began to splinter and one slavering muzzle pushed through, then another, with great teeth wrenching and twisting at the woodwork. They heard Hannibal's hoarse screech, something meaningless but ugly, like 'Boss he say topsides axe crack'. Emily was still trying keys. The Bottle Rabbit took one look at those heaving, slobbering jaws thrusting through the broken door and flung himself in front of Emily with his paws outstretched.

'I won't let them bite you, Emily,' he cried in a rather quavery voice. 'I won't let them hurt you.'

As he spoke there was a rattle behind him. At last the heavy door was open! They were through it in a flash, Emily slamming it shut and locking it again just as the first of the Boxers scrambled, baying, into the long room.

'Boss he say bloodbag, boss he say out out out out out,' the big dog clamoured. But he was too late. Emily and the Bottle Rabbit leant panting against the other side of the locked black door and stared up the white steps to the little tent of blue at the top.

The door was a huge piece of oak. They could hear the Boxers thumping at it already. How long would it last? It was a steep climb. Could they make it in time? And even then, could they escape the pursuit of the vigorous Boxers?

Up the ivory steps they climbed, panting nervously, the lovely pictures now just a blur in the corner of their eyes.

Halfway up – 'Emily. Listen. I think they've stopped, there's no more thumping.'

Both animals paused on one ivory step. Not a sound could be heard below. 'That oak door *is* terribly heavy,' said Emily, 'but we'd better keep going.' And on they scrambled until, hot and breathless, they were out in the sun again.

'Phew,' gasped the rabbit. Never had the green grass and yellow buttercups looked so fresh and welcoming. 'Let's push the white stone thing back – quick!'

13

A joint heave, and it plunked down to shut away that terrible place. They lay on their backs for a long time in the early-morning sun, with buttercups tickling their noses and larks singing overhead.

Then the cat sat up and looked the rabbit in the eye. 'Bottle Rabbit, that was pretty nice of you down there. I mean with the dogs.'

The Bottle Rabbit blushed. 'Oh, it was just something to say, Emily.'

'Well, I thought it was pretty nice.'

The Bottle Rabbit lay there, couldn't think of anything to say now, but actually was tremendously pleased.

After a while Emily murmured, 'Who could believe that such awful dogs existed? So different from Jack and Maisie.' (Emily was calling to mind two dear dog friends of theirs.) 'And I've known some quite nice Boxers, too. Not many, but some. I mean, I was always taught that dogs were a cat's best friend.'

'And a rabbit's best friend,' said the Bottle Rabbit.

'I suppose it was something in their upbringing,' said Emily.

'How do you mean?'

This conversation was interrupted by a polite cough. Standing there was a small, smiling creature about two feet high wearing a black top hat also two feet high. He took off his hat.

'Hello. Me Pob. You come along my house quick. You Bottle Rabbit. You Emily. Yes?'

Both animals were puzzled. 'But how do you know?' asked Emily.

'Golden Baker ol' frien'. Also Golden Eagle ol' frien'. Sam the Bear we all good ol' frien'. Also Fred Charlie famous good horses ol' frien'. Also Golden Baker. Come my house.'

And he courteously waved his superb hat about.

But Emily was looking worried again. 'Pob, Bottle Rabbit, what shall we do? It's almost breakfast-time. Fred and Charlie will be terribly worried. We've been gone all day and all night. They're probably calling out the Golden Eagle yet again, *and* Sam. What shall we do? It's miles back home.'

Now the rabbit stretched his taut woolly body in the calmest way and pulled out his Magic Bottle. It was some time since Emily had seen him so calm and confident.

'Case for the Blue Hares, I think. Better get things moving. I'd better pongle now.' He shook the Bottle, held it some distance from him and said, 'Pongle . . . Pongle . . . Pongle . . . Pongle.' His ears flapped and waved at each pongle.

In what seemed no time at all there came a buzzing and zooming and a neat little blue-and-white aeroplane made a perfect three-point landing. A silver door opened in its side, a staircase came down, and out burst the Six Blue Hares in their smart, shining uniforms.

They lined up and saluted at attention:

'Yes, sir.'

'Yes, sir.'

'Yes, sir.'

'Yes, sir.'

'Yes, sir.'

'Yes, sir, where to, sir?'

'Home please,' said the Bottle Rabbit.

Pob was delightedly waving his magnificent hat about. Emily nudged the Bottle Rabbit. 'Invite him to come too,' she murmured.

'Good idea. Er, Pob, how would you feel about . . . I mean we'd like you to . . . er . . . Emily and I . . .'

'Much happiness, dear creatures,' said the greatly pleased Pob, and the three of them leapt into the plane. The Blue Hares shut the doors, and off they flew.

In the plane they had hot milk and muffins and strawberry jam, and afterwards they played a few rounds of Snap at the card-table; but Emily was still shaken, could not concentrate and kept getting snapped. She stopped playing.

'Those unbelievable Boxers,' she said.

'Yes, and that snobby Voice,' said the Bottle Rabbit.

'I dropped the keys in the rush,' said Emily.

Pob took off his highly polished hat. 'What been going on?'

They told him.

'Thought you looked bothered before.' He put his gleaming hat on again, looking thoughtful. 'Big door, arrowroot biscuits,' he said. 'Yes. Something wrong there, something very bad behind heavy oak door. Best keep away. Some day soon, we – your friends and me – we do something about all that. Bad business, but still you safe and sound.'

'Huzzah,' cried all the Blue Hares, waving their caps.

16

They were about to land just beside Fred and Charlie's little cabin. Blue smoke trailed slowly up from its chimney. They could see a whole group of their friends waiting to greet them, the two cart-horses, the Golden Baker, Sam the Bear with his wife, Maud; the Golden Eagle standing there, and other younger friends hopping about. Fred and Charlie, puffing away at their pipes, looked especially happy. 'Yes, we know, the Blue Hares radioed us from the plane. Tell us later, just rest now,' said Fred, and Charlie nodded. So the animals went straight off for a lie-down.

That evening there was a quiet party, no dancing or anything. Pob did do some tricks, taking things like the ace of spades and pink ribbons out of his profoundly deep hat, and he sang some droll songs in a strange language. Sam the Bear told his usual long jokes, the Eagle told some brief travel yarns, Maud did her imitations. But the Bottle Rabbit and Emily were glad to get to sleep early, and could only mutter their goodnights. They promised Pob they'd go to his house – 'nice friendly good safe house' – soon.

Just before he dropped off to sleep the Bottle Rabbit had one last sleepy word. 'You know, Emily, you know how fond I am of all biscuits? Well, I'm pretty sure from now on I'm off arrowroot, for life ... for life,' he yawned. The rabbit twitched his nose and was asleep. Emily soon dropped off too, quietly purring as the logs crackled in the fireplace and blue smoke rose slowly up the chimney.

17

2

Pob on Land and Water

A few days after the Boxer business the Bottle
Rabbit and Emily decided that a nice quiet
cheering-up thing to do would be going to see
their new friend Pob. He'd left some written
instructions – 'Go to pear tree on hillside by river.
Get blue-white boat there. Row downriver under
the trees – very very nice oh yes' – and so on. It
was a longish walk up a hill and down a hill but in
the end they found the river and found the blue-
and-white boat. It had oars, and a sign on it:

FOR PUBLIC USE ONLY – BY
SUGGESTION, TOWNSHIP OF *YES*.

So in they jumped and soon the Bottle Rabbit was
rowing the boat gently down the stream, merrily
laughing and singing. 'This is the life,' said the
Bottle Rabbit, as Emily dreamily trailed her fine
white paws in the water.

Pretty soon they came to a town with a landing-
stage, thick ropes, bollards, and old animals loun-
ging about. Most wore dark blue jerseys with
'YES' on the front. A notice said 'Welcome to the
Township of YES'. And standing beside it with his
arms flung wide in welcome was that same
smiling creature about two feet high wearing a

black top hat also two feet high – Pob. He raised his magnificent hat.

'Hallo. Come along my house quick.'

They tied up the boat to a bollard and followed Pob, who had put back on his glossy hat. First he introduced them to all the old animals in jerseys. Cat and rabbit shook paws all round.

Then Pob led them to a rose-covered cottage with a thatched roof and flower garden, took off his high hat, ushered them in and sat them down on armchairs.

'Sit down, enjoy comfort,' said Pob, waving his shiny hat about. 'What about some chocolate then?'

'Yes, please, I'd love some,' said Emily.

'Me too,' said the Bottle Rabbit.

'Easy, very easy, just break off bits of chair,' said Pob, suiting the action to the word, breaking

19

off a large chunk of his chair and munching it smilingly.

They tried the same thing, and it worked.

'I've got sort of vanilla flavour here,' said Emily.

'Mine's nuts and raisins.'

'You want plain dark chocolate, use sofa,' spluttered Pob, his mouth full of chocolate cream. 'By the way, thirsty?'

'Well, yes, a bit,' said the Bottle Rabbit.

'Try them taps, any,' said Pob, waving his chimney-pot hat at the kitchen sink, where there were not the usual one or two, but five different taps. 'Try 'em all.'

They got glasses and turned on the taps. Quite amazing really. The first was ginger ale, the second fizzy lemonade, the third ordinary lemonade, the fourth orange juice, the fifth water, for washing glasses and things.

'Got more kinds upstairs in bathroom,' said Pob.

The Bottle Rabbit and Emily had a wonderful time, eating various kinds of chocolate and drinking various kinds of drinks.

'Doesn't the furniture fall to pieces?' asked Emily, eyeing the sofa that they had both been going at pretty hard.

'Yes it does; I get new ones in.'

'Oh.'

When they had had enough for the time being Pob proposed a walk round the town. 'This town called YES. Is very nice place,' he said again. Soon Emily and the Bottle Rabbit found themselves being nodded to and smiled at by every YES citizen they met in the road. All of them greeted the two strangers in the friendliest way.

Everything was like that. They saw a pub. OPEN ALL DAY it said, SINGING, TRAVELLERS WELCOME, and DOGS AND CHILDREN PLEASE COME IN. 'Sounds like a nice pub,' said the Bottle Rabbit. 'Is good pub,' said Pob, 'pub good.' At the entrance to the Town Hall there was a big notice: UNAUTHORIZED PERSONS ONLY. In the park there were signs: KEEP ON THE GRASS, BICYCLING, CAMPING, PICNICKING, and many of the gardens round people's houses had signs: TRESPASSING WILL BE APPRECI-ATED, and BIG KIND DOG IN RESIDENCE. They sat down in a café. SIT WHERE YOU LIKE and DON'T WAIT FOR YOUR TURN and, writ-ten on the menus, NICE FOOD NOT SPECIALLY GOOD FOR YOU. They had ice-cream.

As her delicate pink tongue licked a cone – vanilla and chocolate – Emily's eye fell on a notice-board:

BOOGE PEOPLE CONCERT NEXT WEEK
BEST SEATS FREE
BOOK NOW
ALL SEATS ARE BEST

'You like to go?' asked Pob.

'Oh yes, *please*,' chorused the two animals.

So Pob went to a public telephone, which worked, and soon came back saying, 'Got good news, next week, bring friends.'

More ice-cream was brought to their table. It was all so *pleasant*. The Bottle Rabbit looked round happily. Then a thought struck him. 'Pob, doesn't

21

anything *ever* go wrong here? Doesn't anybody *ever* argue and quarrel and get fed up and everything?'

'Oh my goodness, yes,' said Pob, 'but we do it all on Mondays. Or Moandays, we call them.'

'Moandays?'

'That's what we say. Just ask badgers here. They tell you all about.'

Two attractive young badgers, Margaret and Dorothy, were drinking milk shakes through straws at the next table.

'Tell 'em about Moandays, Margaret, you too, Dorothy,' said Pob.

The two badgers groaned amusingly.

'Oh yes. We call them Moandays all right. That's right. You have to yell and shout and grumble and *moan* at someone that day, get it out of your system for the week, be nasty to someone or be nasty to yourself at least,' said Margaret.

'That's right,' said Dorothy, nodding her head vigorously, 'and *everything* goes wrong on Moanday.

They began to list Moanday miseries, back and forth, taking turns speaking more and more earnestly and faster and faster:

'Rains a lot and too cold.'

'Or too hot and stuffy.'

'Friends say nasty things.'

'*You* say nasty things.'

'Telly goes funny.'

'Fish-and-chip shop closed.'

'Mrs Crutchley comes.'

'Bang your head on the mantelpiece.'

'Lose your specs.'

'Burn the cauliflower.'

'Lose your homework.'

'Boots hurt.'

'Feel fat.'

'Slugs.'

'Earache.'

'Lumpy porridge.'

'No more jam.'

At 'no more jam', the badgers, who had been getting very excited, stopped dead, wiped their brows and eyed one another uncertainly. Emily and the Bottle Rabbit glanced at one another too.

The badgers seemed to be starting up again, more quietly, and looking round the room.

'Uncle Sidney in the park,' muttered Margaret.

'Kick over full paint-tin,' said Dorothy feebly.

'WASPS!' they suddenly shouted with one voice. And then they started to giggle and then they laughed a lot and got up and did a happy dance round and round their café table ('That's a

YES dance,' said Pob). While they danced the badgers sang a very fast lilting song:

> 'Tuesday – Wednesday
> Thursday – Friday
> Saturday – Sunday
> PLANG!
>
> Tuesday – Wednesday
> Thursday – Friday
> Saturday – Sunday
> PLANG!'

They sang it over and over, giving a deft kick of the heels at each 'PLANG!'

When they'd stopped, the Bottle Rabbit cleared his throat. 'What do *you* do on Mon – Moandays, Pob?'

Pob smiled. 'Sleep all day Moanday. Every bit of day and night, get up cheerful on Tuesday.'

'I think I'd do that too.'

Pob leapt up and put on his notable hat. 'Now. Back to water. Time for *Moonbeam*. We go on speedboat now. *Moonbeam* is name of this speedy motorboat.' They said goodbye to Dorothy and Margaret and left the café.

Down at the jetty a blue-and-white speedboat with a brass wheel and leather seats was tied up waiting; all hopped in. Pob started the engine and twirled the wheel. He had to hold it one-handed as his other hand was holding on to his stove-pipe hat and they were chugging along quite fast. The pensive Emily, reclined, gazed on the stream below, and also on the greenish-creamy waves

24

that their wake spread wide across the river, rattling the boats moored along its banks. The Bottle Rabbit, however, ears flapping in the breeze, stared happily ahead. The river was full of surprising bends and they wobbled about quite a lot with Pob's one-handed steering. 'Is easy, this!' he cried. 'Just keep straight ahead – whoops – ' Pob swerved round some cheerful ducks – 'no problem, just keep – werps!' He narrowly missed two ferrets in a canoe.

The Bottle Rabbit loved this kind of messing about in boats. Pob had gradually got control of the *Moonbeam* and they'd travelled quite a few miles down the beautiful river under the overarching trees when he turned, smiling, 'You like to try?' The rabbit leapt forward eagerly. 'Be careful, Bott—' began Emily, but the words died on her lips when KLONK – KLONK – KLONK – the engine stopped, the rabbit pushed at the starter-button, the boat drifted silently on.

'Klonk?' the Bottle Rabbit now said to himself, 'where have I heard that before?' Then he clapped paw to brow. 'Ooops! That's the Bugatti noise.' He was remembering a bad time he'd once had when Ken the Pig had got him to swap his Magic Bottle for a big old car that didn't go.

Meanwhile, Pob for once was looking bothered as he pushed and pulled at various instruments, even trying something with a piece of string. Nothing happened except that just once the boat-engine went 'BARRUMPH!' But then it klonked again and remained silent. Two swans, their wide wings thung-ing and thung-ing, flew high over their heads.

'At least we're still moving,' said the Bottle Rabbit cheerfully.

'Yes, quite rapidly, too,' said Emily quietly.

'Hm. Yes. Ouch! *Moan*! Oh ... Moanday. Moanday!' shouted Pob in a loud voice. He was staring ahead to where a watery mist rose high into the trees and a loud roaring struck the air. It was a weir – a kind of wide waterfall where the untamed and intractable river went seething and bubbling and crashing down ten feet at least on to craggy rocks below. And now they were racing towards it quite out of control, with leaves and sticks eddying round them.

'Good Lord,' said the Bottle Rabbit.

Emily looked pale. 'What can we do?' her white tail waved stiffly.

'Can't get the moaning thing going – no way to stop this *Moanbeam*,' gasped Pob, whose tall hat had fallen off.

The boat was careering sideways now, nearer and nearer to disaster. The Bottle Rabbit waved his paws about disconsolately. How could they escape crashing down the weir, messing up the boat, ruining Pob's hat, perhaps getting crushed and drowned, perhaps even losing his Magic Bottle?

Then. An astonishing thing. PLOOMF! From the riverbank a heavily-built and powerful-looking pig-body was heaving towards them through the racing water using a butterfly stroke that pushed his head bouncily in and out of the river. The Bottle Rabbit heard a bubbling, grunting shout, 'Hold on tight old man! Ken's on the case! Put your trust in Ken!'

The weir was now only feet away. At one
moment they could feel the shining smooth cruel
falling water pulling them ever nearer the dangerous edge, and the next – THUMP BUMP CLUMP –
and Ken's big wet head was butting and nosing
their boat towards the bank. They could see all
four of his trotters paddling fiercely against the
stream. 'Somebody get that brush working! Row
with the brush!' they heard him grunt breath-
lessly. Emily caught on. She picked up a yard-
brush that lay in the scuppers and, plunging its
head in the surging river, she rowed and rowed as
hard as she could towards the bank. Ken's big
pig-head and the charming white cat's rowing
brush together did the trick. The boat scraped into
some creaking bulrushes with only inches to go.

27

Pob leapt ashore with the painter and secured it to a tree-stump, the other two jumped after him – and all were safe. The moored boat tugged in the fast-flowing stream as the weir roared on. Now light rain began to fall.

'Went and got your engine seized up, didn't you? Where's your blooming oil then? Rank carelessness *I* call it.' A surly weasel, with 'Frank's Body Shop' written across his front, growled all this at them from behind a tree. But the animals ignored him; their eyes were on the large pig. With splodgings and bloochings a bedraggled Ken was clambering up the muddy bank, his three-piece suit a soggy mess, his boots waterlogged. He snorted and panted and stared downstream where a pork-pie hat went eddying and thrusting along.

'There she goes,' he wheezed as his hat bobbed unheeded on the wake of the swells. 'Always kind of liked that tweed job. Looked sporty on me I always thought. Amazing how it keeps afloat. Well, so it goes. Up one day, down the next. Bucket in a well. You win some, you lose some.' He sneezed and grinned all at one go.

The three animals grinned at him as hard as they could. 'That was really brave, Ken,' said Emily. 'You – you saved our lives.'

'*And* my Magic Bottle,' said the Bottle Rabbit.

'Very, very, *very* good,' said Pob.

Ken sneezed again. 'My pleasure. Be my guest. Just happened to be there. Saw the prob. All in the day's . . .' Ken then staggered forward in the wet mud. 'Here, what's going on? What's the idea?'

It was just Sam the Bear, who had loomed up behind him and slapped him approvingly on the shoulder with a heavy paw.

'Steady on, old man,' said Ken, grinning warily. 'Mind my back. Only one I've got you know.' He straightened himself up and winked at Emily, 'You all right, flower?' He winked at the Bottle Rabbit, 'No bones broken, old man?' And he winked at Pob, 'Held on to *your* hat all right then, eh? When all the rest had flown?' He was now nudging Pob rather forcefully in the ribs, but Pob didn't seem to mind one bit, just smoothed his vast hat. Ken looked over his shoulder at Sam again. 'You do keep turning up, don't you, old man? Rain or shine?'

But by now Sam was clasping Ken's trotter in his massive paw and pumping it up and down in congratulation. 'Splendid work, Ken. I saw it all. An admirable action. We owe you an immense debt of gratitude.' And Sam settled in to one of his speeches, mostly proposing that a banquet of honour, presided over by himself, should be held as a reward for Ken in the Town Hall of YES; but also praising Ken at length, 'Resourceful pig . . . magnanimous pig . . .' At a pause in this flowing speech, Ken managed to interrupt.

'Don't give it another thought, old man,' he said. 'Comes a time a pig has to do what a pig has to do. But to tell the truth, old man, if you're talking rewards I don't mind saying a quick whip-round would suit me more than a banquet.' Ken raised a trotter. 'Don't get me wrong, old man. Don't want to put a damper on your knees-up; but the fact is I'm a bit short this week and any little

29

something would come in handy. Just to tide me over. Got a wife and three kids to support, you know, payments due on the old wagon, under the doctor with my chest, water on the knee . . .' Ken sneezed again and hopped about; his little tail was wiggling and wiggling.

'Oh. Quite so. Perfectly reasonable idea. I'll make it my business to visit every home in the forest this weekend and see what can be done. Meanwhile, pray do accept this small token . . .' The good-natured bear slipped a banknote from his wallet and handed it to Ken who promptly shoved it into a moist pocket.

'Thanks a lot, Sam, I appreciate that. Well, I reckon I'll be oozing along. See you folks around. Got to see a mackerel about a cod.' And Ken sauntered squelching off, looking cheerful enough. His pig-music sounded muffled this time, more like pig-sneezes, fading away through the forest. By now it was pouring down and the animals took shelter in a shed.

'Extraordinary animal, Ken,' said Sam, shaking his head. 'The things he comes out with. Wife . . . chest . . . knee. Ken isn't married, as we well know, and he's fit as a fiddle. Yes. Something of a rough diamond, our Ken, on the outside. But there's a heart of gold in there. Yes, if you care to dig you'll find a silver lining in that pig.'

'I've always liked Ken very much,' said the Bottle Rabbit softly.

With a sigh he reached for his Magic Bottle and stared after the departing pig. 'Ken really saved this for me when he rescued us from the weird,' he whispered to Emily; and then louder, 'Ken really is a Kind Animal.' As he spoke he was polishing the Bottle on his taut woolly body. 'Perhaps I should let him have a go with it. He does love it. Yes, I'll give him a go.' And he hopped off into the woods. 'Ken,' he shouted, 'Ken! Come back, Ken!'

Ken instantly reappeared, dripping and snorting. 'You spoke, old man?'

The rabbit was holding out the Bottle to him. 'Ken you must think me awfully unkind after you being so brave saving us and everything and me not letting you even have a go at the Bottle I mean.'

'Not my place, old man,' said Ken, panting. 'Mind you, I could use a sandwich or two, not to mention a drop of the old brand – I mean a nice glass or two of lemonade.'

The rabbit pressed his precious Magic Bottle into Ken's trotter. 'Please have a go, Ken.' He looked round at his friends. 'We all want you to, don't we?' The other animals nodded glumly.

'This on the level? OK. Will do. Thanks much.' Ken was clearly astonished, but his little eyes sparkled as he uncorked the dark green Bottle, trotters trembling. For a moment he hesitated, looking almost shy, then he pongled hard once. 'Pongle,' he said, firmly, then again, twice, 'Pongle, pongle.'

Within minutes a lovely spread of chicken sandwiches, egg sandwiches, cheese and tomato sandwiches and small pies had arrived, wrapped as ever in spotless white napkins with the usual cutlery and silver pots of mustard and mayonnaise. A minute later a jeremiah of ice-cold lemonade

31

had plumped down.

Ken was beside himself with delight. 'A pongle! I don't believe it! I've done an all-time, genuine pongle!' He began a triumphant comic polka, back and forth on the tips of his trotters, his front-legs held up like a ballerina's arms. 'Callooh! Callay!' he chortled. 'I gloat, I gloat – hear me!' And he performed little twinkling pirouettes and twirls while the others laughed and applauded. At last, flushed and beaming, he sank down on a bench. The animals had never seen him so simply happy, and they all gathered round him to munch and gulp and chat. The rain had stopped, the sun was out.

Yet such happiness rarely lasts long. Ken soon grew strangely quiet. The pig was knitting his brows. By and by his little tail had begun to twiddle again; he got up, paced about, turned and spoke. 'Lovely grub, that, beats anything they dish you out at the club. Well folks, you'll excuse me a moment, I've just got to – back in a sec.' And Ken slipped off into the trees with a funny look on his face.

A dark thought had serpented into his mind and his heart was thumping excitedly. 'Now I can pongle I'll get the Six Blue Hares to land by the river. I'll get them to fly me off. It's only fair. I *need* it, I mean, share and share alike. And what's to stop me? I'll try the Costa del Sol, a nice condo – lots of sun, no trouble, brandy, cigars. Send him back the Bottle later.'

Gabbling away like this the pig stepped behind an aspen tree and pongled five times: PONGLE ... PONGLE ... PONGLE ... PONGLE ... PONGLE

– then waited. No result. The aspen quivered. He
tried again, again nothing happened. Ken's neck
bulged and sweated. 'OINGKH,' he cried,
'OINGKH.' Then came the inevitable, a shadow
hung over him and Sam the Bear was there.
'Kindness, Ken, Kindness,' murmured Sam. 'You
must strive to remember what is inscribed upon
that Bottle you are holding:

> This Truth ever bear in Mind
> I'm only useful to the Kind.'

He held out his huge black paw.

'Pipped at the post again,' grumbled Ken as he
gave up the Bottle. 'It's all right for some.' He
grunted a little. 'Oh well, there it is. We pigs seem
born for pain.' He scratched his head, hummed a

33

sad little ditty. Then, 'Look, Sam, that rabbit likes me a lot. I know he does. And I like him too. Could we just keep this one quiet? I don't think he noticed. He doesn't notice.'

Sam frowned and pursed his lips, then nodded, 'Hm, yes, I take your point. Yes. Let us treat this as a momentary lapse, shall we? And what the Bottle Rabbit doesn't know won't hurt him. Indeed. Yes. A good thought, Ken.'

The two animals shook hands solemnly, then bear and chastened pig walked back. As they walked, Sam harrumphed once or twice and then: 'I'm afraid this means no banquet, Ken, and no speech from me, though we might manage a rather small honorarium.'

Ken said nothing.

Back in the hut, Pob and Emily sighed in relief as the two came in, but the Bottle Rabbit just grinned cheerfully as Sam handed him back his Bottle.

'Come to my house everybodies hot cocoa,' said Pob suddenly. 'Forget boat trouble, any trouble, get dry.'

'Yes, indeed. I understand you keep cocoa on tap at all times, Pob,' said Sam the Bear. 'Let us all go there. Coming are you, Ken?'

'Warm cocoa did you say? And very nice, too. But the fact is I'm expected down at the . . . got a chap waiting . . . better be on my way. So long, all. Have a good one.' And Ken hurriedly splodged off. The Bottle Rabbit waved and waved after him for some time. Ken didn't sing a single note.

Then the other animals all climbed on to Sam's back and in a few dozen of that splendid bear's

strides they were back at Pob's where Sam, Emily,
the Bottle Rabbit, Margaret, Dorothy, and Pob
himself spent a restful hour, getting dry, drinking
hot cocoa and nibbling furniture. Sam took a nip
of something stronger in his cocoa.

As she sat there, Emily got very interested in
Pob's clock hanging on the wall. She thought it
was probably made out of a round iced tart with
chocolate hands, but thought it better not to find
out as she was pretty full. Then she saw that the
clock said ten-past-nine.

'I think we should be getting back home, you
know. It'll be getting dark soon, even though it's
summer.' She pointed at the clock.

'Is not quite so late,' said Pob, 'is only eight
o'clock. I eat that clock at night a lot. Make it go
fast.'

'How enormously interesting,' said Sam. 'Still, I
think it is bedtime all round rather soon. Off we
go I think.'

And after many goodbyes to Pob ('No bedtime
in YES,' Pob managed to whisper to the Bottle
Rabbit), Sam took the cat and rabbit home.

Back in the cabin in front of the fire, the two
great stamping shaggy-fetlocked cart-horses, Fred
and Charlie, listened carefully to the young
animals' amazing stories, taking a special interest
in their account of Ken the Pig's quick thinking,
courage, and determination.

'Good old Ken, then,' said Fred at last, 'always
count on a pig in an emergency. And I like the
sound of YES,' he went on. 'Pity everywhere can't
be like that. Pob, Moandays and all. YES, is it?
Should suit Sam too . . . That right, Charlie?'

Charlie puffed on his pipe and nodded in agreement.

Later, as the Bottle Rabbit settled down to sleep by the fire with his Magic Bottle safely in his pocket, he found himself wondering about the *Moonbeam*. 'I expect I'll be able to have a go with it some other time, when it's mended,' he thought. 'And I'm really glad I let Ken have a go with my Bottle. He liked it so much and he's so nice.' Then he wondered sleepily whether Ken liked music at all. It would be nice to invite him to the Booge People's concert at YES. After all, he'd been a really heroic pig this afternoon. But would Ken like Booge music? Anyhow, what exactly *was* a Booge – a Booo – a Boogaloo – a Booogalloogallooo – ? Gently mouthing these strange words the young rabbit drifted off like a little boat into a calm sleep, as did Emily, the visiting Margaret and Dorothy, and every other animal in Fred and Charlie's peaceful cabin.

3

Dancing in the Beech Grove

One late-summer morning Fred was working steadily in a shady beech grove not far from the cabin. He was splitting logs with a wedge and sledgehammer, making a woodpile for next winter. The scent of resin hung sweet and heavy in the air and the grove was warm and still.

Fred was humming and singing an old tune to himself – 'Cherry Ripe' actually – when his ears caught the sound of another animal with a high voice raised in peculiar song; long, lilting and thoughtful, with a curious sinking note at the end of each line.

'Once animals in Australia, who wanted a good
   beard,
Had a very curious way of getting one, it
   appeared.
Pricked their chins all over with a pointed bone,
Stroked them very carefully with a magic stick or
   stone.
This thing represented a long-whiskered type of
   rat –
The virtue of the whiskers was transferred and
   that was that.
Shall we say what sort of lesson this kind of story
   gives?

Yes. One HALF of the world CAN'T know how
the OTHER really lives.
Have I said what kind of lesson this sort of story
gives?
Yes. One HALF of the world CAN'T know how
the OTHER really lives.'

It was an armadillo quietly singing, and as she
ended her song she did a little jig, her long, supple, armour-plated body weaving about, her little
feet pattering. Fred rested his axe carefully and
watched her. After a while she stopped.

Fred moved towards her, hefting his axe. 'I say,
that's an interesting song you've been singing. I'd
like to hear it again,' said the cart-horse.

So the armadillo sang it again, and did the little jig again. 'I'm glad you like it. It's about magic, you know. We armadillos have always been sympathetic to magic.' She did another little skip. 'But then I imagine you Clydesdales must know all that kind of stuff very well, too – grew up with tree-spirits and corn-gods and magic circles, I expect.'

'Well, not really,' said Fred.

The singer and dancer was one of the fairground armadillos who'd come in from the West, a quiet, well-bred-looking animal with a friendly smile and a modest air, though she *was* wearing an emerald-green waistcoat and a bright yellow flouncy skirt – her funfair get-up – over her extraordinary armour-plated body. Her tail waved cheerfully as she chanted the last line for the third time: 'Yes, one HALF of the world CAN'T know how the OTHER really lives.' She shook a little sequinned handbag at the word 'lives'.

Fred was resting an elbow on the haft of his great axe and mulling over what the armadillo had sung. After a while he shook his head. 'Can't say I understand what it's on about. But I like the song, especially the pointed bone and virtue business. And beards have always interested me greatly. Care for a cup of tea or a gulp of beer?'

'Thanks. I'd really like some beer. Thirsty work, chanting these old ditties, and then there's the dancing. We armadillos are all singers and dancers, you know.'

'No. I didn't know that,' said Fred. 'Well, you live and learn.' And shaking his head amiably he went off to his cabin. Soon he was back with his own big pewter tankard and a nicely decorated glass mug for the armadillo. Both vessels brimmed over with foaming beer.

'Just the thing,' said the armadillo, and the two of them sat down on a log in the shady grove, musing and nursing their beer. They hadn't a lot to say to one another, but just got on well, sitting there saying nothing very special.

'Been in Australia, then?' said Fred.

'No. Just heard about it.'

'They say there's a lot going on down there we don't know about.'

'I'm sure you're right.'

'Look,' said Fred, 'if you're interested in odd goings-on perhaps you'd like to come with some of us on an expedition we're planning.' He gave the armadillo a brief glance with his big kindly horse-eyes. 'It's not going to be entirely safe, mind you. We might run into some trouble. You see, we've decided we've got to deal with the Voice and his Boxers once and for all. It's now or never. And we need another smallish animal.'

'You've got to deal with the what and his what?'

'The Voice and his Boxers. It's pretty complicated. We'll be going behind the heavy door, you know. Or some of us will.'

'Heavy . . .?'

'Look. I'll get Pob; Pob's the one who knows most about it. Wait here and I'll get Pob. Did the beards really grow when they did that stroking out in Australia? Well, don't tell me now, I'll get Pob.' Fred trotted off again and soon came galloping back with a funny little smiling person bobbing up and down on his broad brown back.

He was about two feet tall and wore a hat that was also two feet high. It was Pob. He spoke fast.

'Hello, I'm Pob. You Fred's frien' my frien'. Fred Charlie Golden Baker all good ol' frien'. Bottle Rabbit Emily Golden Eagle Golden Baker . . .'

'Yes, yes, Pob. That's all right, we're all friends,' Fred broke in. 'And this is a new friend – by the way, I'm sorry, I don't know your name.'

The armadillo hung her head shyly. 'I'm called Daisy-puss, I'm afraid,' she hesitated. 'It's an old armadillo name.'

'What's wrong with Daisy-puss?' cried Fred stoutly. 'It's a nice name. Unusual.' He was rather taken with this armadillo.

'Good name. All frien's got good name, like me,' said Pob.

'Well, tell Daisy-puss about the Boxers and the heavy door,' said Fred. 'And the Voice too. She knows a lot about magic sticks and stones,' he added.

'Actually, my friends all call me Daisy,' said the armadillo.

'Then Daisy it shall be. Go ahead, Pob.'

So Pob explained about the white stairs that led down to a fancy room and how animals were lured there and then imprisoned by a gang of fierce Boxers who robbed them and maltreated them and how the Boxers were directed by an arrogant Voice over loudspeakers and how nobody had ever seen the Voice just heard it and how the Bottle Rabbit and Emily had once been caught and had had a narrow escape. Pob stopped for breath and Fred broke in: 'So we're going

41

along to see what we can do. Care to come?'

'I'd love to,' said Daisy who had been listening with great attention. 'I might just have a trick or two up my sleeve for these unpleasant-sounding creatures. For one thing, I've a very fair idea of what we can expect when we meet the Voice.' Daisy, no longer shy, spoke rapidly and firmly, ticking off points on one of her front feet. 'The reports of your friend Emily and – the *Bottle* Rabbit, is it? Curious name, that – clearly point to the presence of some obese or bedridden buffalo or bison with a grudge against society, or simply consumed by overwhelming greed. Now your average buffalo can be a very single-minded fellow. As I see it, this one will be sitting beside a microphone and staring into his spying device, a closed circuit television. I say buffalo because your friends report *smiling* dogs and *laughing* buffaloes in the wall-paintings on those white stairs. In my view it's all part of a fiendish plan. We have these fierce and scowling dogs in real life. We may now, then, expect a real and scowling and very wealthy buffalo; don't you agree? Yes. We'll find a buffalo down there.'

Daisy paused. Fred stared at her admiringly. 'How do you do it, Daisy? I must say I would never have thought of the Voice as a buffalo.'

'Elementary, my dear Fred,' said the armadillo. 'Put two and two together and you get the inevitable four.'

'Ahem! Ahem!' A breathless little voice spoke high above in a maple. But Fred and Daisy and Pob were so absorbed in their plans that nobody noticed little Count Hubert counting up in the tree.

'Well, none of us likes that lot. Too much money for their own good; they're really a disgrace to the forest, hurting animals and taking their stuff,' said Fred. 'Charlie and I and Sam the Bear would be down there after them ourselves, but we're too big, you see. You can only get at them down those narrow white steps or through this little white door Pob knows about. I'm so glad you want to do this, Daisy. And really pleased you have some tricks up your sleeve.'

'My sleeve full of tricks too,' said Pob. 'All come my house now.' So Pob hopped on Fred's back and the speedy armadillo ran by his side as the horse galloped calmly off, head up, his great furred hooves battering the sandy pathway to Pob's.

So Daisy and Fred discovered the remarkable cottage that Pob lived in. He ushered them in, invited them to sit down, offered them chocolate.

'Chocolate!' exclaimed Daisy with relish. 'I just can't say no. All we armadillos have a sweet tooth.'

'Break off a piece of chair, sofa, sideboard. All varieties. Want drink? Go to taps.' And Daisy discovered the marvels of the edible furniture and the taps that poured lemonade, ginger beer and so many other drinks. While she was breaking off pieces of furniture and sipping lemonade and while Fred smoked his pipe, Pob explained the trick he had up his sleeve, and Daisy explained hers.

Soon the three of them walked down to the dock and climbed into Pob's blue-and-white speedboat, the *Moonbeam*. They chugged off up the river, Pob at the wheel with his high-grade hat at a rakish angle, Fred standing four-square and firm in the middle of the boat, Daisy's long nose pointing up and out over the bows as she enjoyed the river breeze.

They came to a pear tree, laden with clusters of burgeoning fruit, and tied the boat to it. Then the three friends strolled across the long hot fields to a bank overgrown in a tangle of ferns and bracken where Pob found the little white door. 'Quiet. Listen,' he said. They stood still, and presently above all the live murmur of a summer's day they could hear a tiny voice softly singing: 'Humble bumble key, humble bumble key. Ah yes. Humble bumble key.' Pob pointed to a rocky ledge above the white door, and Fred reached up and took down a small silver key. Its singing stopped when he picked it up.

'This one, Pob?'

Pob turned to him. 'Fred. Need cart. For dogs. Please get. We go in. You too big here.'

'What cart?'

'Any cart. For Boxers.'

'Right then,' said Fred. 'You watch yourself, Daisy,' he added, smiling as he ambled off.

Pob looked back with some regret at the green fields and blue skies. He didn't much cherish the thought of going into this danger. But he unlocked the white door, entered with Daisy, locked it behind him, pocketed the key and turned and looked up the long flight of ivory-white steps climbing up into the hill.

'Notice the paintings, Pob,' said Daisy, peering up. 'Dogs *and buffaloes*.'

'Is very beautiful,' said Pob with a sigh.

44

Now they took deep breaths and pushed firmly at that heavy oaken door. It opened easily, as it had for Emily and the Bottle Rabbit, and again, above the hothouse flowers and dishes carelessly displayed, were the same inviting notices that cat and rabbit had responded to. Pob and Daisy walked in and sat down watchfully on a sofa.

'What next?' said Pob. They hadn't long to wait.

'What's this I see?' bellowed someone. '*More* impertinent animals making free with my property? I shall not stand for it. Who are *you* there, with the grotesque headwear? And my God, what on earth is that thing with you? What do you mean by bursting into private premises in this uncouth fashion?' The arrogant Voice was there again.

'It *says* "welcome" here . . .' began Daisy in a quiet voice.

'Silence, Madam. I am *not* – repeat, *not* – interested in the remotest way in anything either of you could possibly wish to say to me. Is that perfectly understood? Wait there in silence. We know how to deal with your sort, by Jove. Oh yes.' The Voice laughed harshly. 'We know exactly what to do, you sam. All right, Hannibal, get to work. And make it hot for them. And see that you get that jewelled handbag while you're about it, will you?'

Then came that same awful clamouring and grunting as the Boxers, led by long-legged Hannibal, burst yelping into the room. Before they could say 'Jack Robinson', Pob and Daisy were surrounded, bundled down the corridor and thrust into that same cage. A gate clanged, a key turned, and they were prisoners. The Boxers, lean and heaving, panting and drooling, loped about, staring at them. Big Hannibal was already nosing into Daisy's glittering handbag.

But the brutal dogs were not going to have it all their own way. The joint plan was now put into effect. Pob, standing well back in the cage, removed his tall hat and took a large box of chocolates, with a coloured picture of flowers on it, out of its crown. He opened the box, selected a chocolate, dandled it, and pretended to munch it. 'Soft centres. Yum, yum,' he said loudly, fondling his plump stomach. The Boxers all growled and started drooling more heavily than before. Pob began to flip chocolates at them. The dogs leapt on their hind-legs and snapped them up, their throats straining and their pink jaws clashing. They scrambled and jostled one another in the most unmannerly way, but Pob saw to it that they all got plenty of chocolates – except one Boxer – their leader, Hannibal. Hannibal growled and yelped, his brindled muzzle nosing through the bars of their prison-cage.

'Gimme chockluck. Boss say you gimme chockluck plenty quick,' he yelped abysmally, drool dripping from his slavering jaws.

Daisy was waiting for Hannibal. Armadillos are harmless, inoffensive creatures: but Daisy, who liked her sequinned handbag very much, was now extremely irritated. She spun round, and with a loud 'Dai!' whipped her long tail through the bars and across the big dog's back. Then, 'Yah!' With a fierce blow she had Hannibal pinned against the cell gate. 'We armadillos are all skilled

46

in karate,' she panted. 'I'll get his keys. Pob, give him the chocolates.' Hannibal yelped and snapped at her with his strong white teeth, but Daisy's armadillo armour was proof against his angry bites, and her clenched tail held him fast. As she pulled the keys off his leather belt and also retrieved her sequinned handbag, Pob nipped nimbly up and stuffed a handful of chocolates into the scoundrelly animal's open jaws.

Now a strange scene was enacted. The Boxers' shattering yells began to sound gentler, snarls became yawns, yelps became snores. Boxer after Boxer dropped to the floor, one leathery body after another sliding down, limbs splayed in unsightly fashion as sleep overtook each beast. Last to go was Hannibal. 'Boss he say topsides blong chockluck leg before wicket . . .' But by now his bark was a puppylike 'bow wow, bow wow', as big Hannibal slumped to the ground with the others. Daisy and Pob stared at each other contentedly; the plan was working.

'Dogs quiet now three four hours,' said Pob, as he helped Daisy unlock the gate. 'Special dopey chocolate work good.'

'Nice job,' said Daisy. 'Now for the Voice.'

'Now for the Voice indeed.' It came crackling out of the loudspeakers. 'How *dare* you? Don't you dare move one inch. Back into your cell, and quick about it. I – I have twenty more dogs up here, not one of them a chocolate-lover. *And* there's an untamed cougar waiting for you. D-don't move, I say. St-stay where you are, you – you – rotters.' The voice still bayed arrogantly, but there was a nervous edge to it now.

47

'What do you think, Daisy?' said Pob.

'I think we have that buffalo on the run. It's a risk, but let's face it.'

'Me too. Let's go,' said Pob.

Pob squared his shoulders and straightened his huge hat. Daisy took another deep breath, and the two of them walked out of the cage, down the corridor, into the long silver-grey room, and started towards the door the Boxers had come in at.

'I said stay where you are, you frightful bounders, you. Go home. G-go away. L-leave my property at once or I'll set my b-bulldogs and Alsatian police-dogs at your throats.' There was panic in the Voice now.

'Bluffing,' said Pob.

'Yes. Who does that buffalo think we are? We armadillos never surrender,' said Daisy firmly.

They flung open that door and strode into the next room. What a strange scene! As Daisy had foretold, there was a television set and there was a microphone, in fact a battery of microphones. However – to their amazement – crouching behind them was not a fierce bedridden buffalo, only a small, trembling, long-whiskered type of rat, thin-featured with thin lips. This rat was elegantly dressed for country living; tweeds, deerstalker hat, shooting stick, riding breeches, polished leather gaiters. They stared at him.

'So you the thief and bully,' said Pob.

The trembling rat seemed to cower in front of them as he crossed his wrists: 'I'll come quietly. I – I surrender. I won't give any trouble. Just keep that armadillo away from me, that's all.' He'd

48

evidently watched Daisy dealing with Hannibal on his closed-circuit television set. Pob nodded curtly. The rat jumped up and spoke fast. 'L-look. You can have all my stuff. Just leave me alone. I'll – I'll give you all my stuff, stocks and shares, too – everything. All right? Is that all right? F-follow me, it's all in the garden.'

'Very very well,' said Pob, 'but make snappy.'

The rat led them to another door, opened it and stepped aside. Pob and Daisy moved out into the yard surrounded by high stone walls built into the side of the hill. In one corner was stacked a staggering heap of stuff: telescopes, string bags, basket chairs, false beards, stamp albums, brown-paper parcels, axes, Australian beer-mugs, boxing gloves, gum-shoes, galoshes, knee-boots, a toy stuffed buffalo, a bundle of pointed sticks and stones, two guillemot's eggs, a miniature Connemara bog-oak tripod-stand . . . Pob and Daisy

49

were utterly absorbed with these things until they heard a door clank shut and a key turn, and the sound of pattering feet scuffling away.

'Well, I'll be . . .' began Pob.

The gentleman rat had tricked them after all. They were imprisoned again between these stone walls.

'Don't worry. Watch this,' said Daisy, who had been rather quiet since they had found a rat and no buffalo. She now flung herself to the ground and dug her long head into it. Earth flew up all round her. Within moments there was a sizeable hole. In five minutes, as Pob watched open-mouthed, she had disappeared into the tunnel she had made. Daisy reappeared for a moment. 'We armadillos have always been notable bur-rowers,' she gasped cheerfully. Then she got back down to it, nose, tail and all four feet working away. In no time there was a tunnel right under the wall so that Pob, his mighty hat off, could squeeze through with ease. Minutes later they had found their way back to the pear tree and to Fred, who was waiting there patiently with a brewery cart. He was humming and singing in his quiet way:

> 'Cherry ripe, cherry ripe,
> Ripe, ripe I cry-y,
> Full and fair ones
> Co-o-o-ome and buy-y.
> Cherry ripe, cherry ripe . . .'

Fred broke off. 'Any troubles?' he asked, and then, bewilderedly, 'but how on earth did you get out? The little white door's still closed.'

'No time. Tell you soon. Got to get dogs,' said
Pob.

He and Daisy disappeared back through the
white door, back through the heavy door, and
back to the cell, where they began lugging Boxer
after snoring Boxer out into the open and, with
Fred's help, dumped dog after inanimate dog into
the brewer's cart. Last to come was Hannibal. A
heavy job tugging and pulling his big leathery
body out and squeezing him through the white
door, and tumbling him head-over-heels on top of
the others. Hannibal half stirred and half opened
a bloodshot eye, and half muttered, 'Boss he say
stumped', then sank back into slumber. Pob's
special chocolates were powerful medicine.

Daisy and Pob hopped on to the driver's bench
and Fred quietly lumbered back to the cabin.
Everybody was there when they arrived: Charlie,
the Golden Baker and his three sisters, the Golden
Eagle, Count Hubert, Emily and the Bottle Rabbit,
many young animals, and in the middle, seated
on a large stone, with Maud at his side, the majes-
tic and reassuring figure of Sam the Bear. The
assembly was astonished to see a creaking cartload of snoring Boxers approaching. But there was
a burst of applause, led by Fred, as first Daisy
then Pob leapt down from the cart bench.

'This is my friend Daisy,' said Fred, beaming.
'She's come to visit us and she's just done this
brave thing with Pob. She's . . . she's an armadillo.' All the animals applauded some more; Fred
looked extremely pleased.

It was four o'clock now, and Charlie, who had

cooked up a mammoth bowl of chilli, set it out in front of the cabin, with lemonade for the younger and beer for the older animals. All partook heartily.

Over this late lunch a debate began on what to do about Hannibal and the other Boxers. As usual, Sam found the solution. 'They must be split up,' he said. 'We must find good homes for each of them. Individually they are probably good enough poor brutes, if properly looked after. They may very well never have had the advantages of a decent home life. Amazing that one small rat could dominate them so effectively, and bend them to his evil will. An aristoc-rat, I suppose?' All the animals laughed politely; Sam did not often make jokes. 'However that may be,' he went on, 'Fred and Charlie and I will take them off into the forest and make inquiries and find some sensible well-disciplined homes (there must be firmness) where each of them can be placed. Perhaps with some honest Boxer families.'

Everyone agreed that this was the solution ('I'm not sure about that Hannibal, mind you,' the Bottle Rabbit whispered to Emily), as Sam and the Clydesdales prepared to leave.

'What about the Voice, Sam? You know, the buff – the Rat, rather?' asked Fred.

Daisy went a little pink around the cheeks. 'Oh, I imagine he'll show us a clean pair of heels,' said Sam. 'Without his Boxers he won't have a leg to stand on. He'll toe the line from now on. My informed guess, and believe me, I have some experience in these matters, is that he'll foot it; we won't catch sight or sound of him in this neighbourhood, if he knows which side his bread is buttered on.' Sam smiled, and the other animals smiled back politely. The bear ended with a long-ish speech in praise of Pob and Daisy's initiative, and outlined arrangements for the return of all the property that the Rat had taken from other animals.

That evening a band of nine brilliantly-costumed armadillos arrived and threw a party for Daisy and her new friends in the beech grove. They set up a multitude of torches and in their ruddy glare two of the armadillos appeared bearing cakes served piping hot on a bed of leaves, also hot sausages on sticks, and, an armadillo speciality, barbecued bones on pointed stones. All ate heartily, until it became time for the armadillos to move into their dance. Forming a wide circle they started a grunting and rhythmic stamping, and then began to run. They ran weaving and inter-weaving round and round in the grove, faster and faster, their little feet scuttling and kicking, their

knees lifting higher and higher as they gathered speed.

'I suppose it's all a sort of elaborate karate practice,' Fred said to Charlie in an aside. Charlie grinned and nodded. 'Daisy's especially agile, isn't she?' said Fred. Charlie nodded again.

The rhythmic grunting and stamping grew louder and louder, and strangely intense. And then the armadillos began to sing in shrill unison:

'Knees, knees, glorious knees,
  Make up a parcel of buffaloes' knees.
  Stop a bit –
  Think a bit –
  Tangle the string a bit –
  Go to the bank and surrender your knees.
  Knees, knees, glorious knees – '

They sang it fast and rhythmically, stamping their feet as they ran, repeating it more and more loudly and excitedly, their knees rising higher and faster.

  'Knees, knees, glorious knees,
   Make up a parcel of buffaloes' knees.
   Clank a bit –
   Clang a bit –
   Fondle and dandle it –
   Out with you, up with you, relish those knees.
   Knees, knees, glorious knees – '

  Again and again it came. The armadillos were now throwing themselves about abandonedly as they danced, waving their heads in delirious happiness. 'Join in! Join in!' they cried ecstatically. 'All join in!'

  'Knees, knees, glorious knees,
   Make up a parcel of buffaloes' knees.
   Stroke a bit –
   Prick a bit –
   Stone it and stick at it –
   Cherish that parcel, Oh cherish those knees.
   Knees, knees, glorious knees – '

  Soon the whole crowd was leaping around, the Eagle and the Baker, Pob, Emily and the Bottle Rabbit, Maud of course, and even Sam the Bear, who joined in, hopping spiritedly, his great black furry head nodding. Charlie was there, and Fred joined up with Daisy as all of them went surging and swaying and chanting; and so they continued until late into the warm night, when gradually everyone sank exhausted to the ground and slept where they lay in the beech grove. And later the armadillos quietly gathered themselves together, quietly whispered a joint goodbye and quietly pattered off under the scent-laden beech boughs. And Daisy cast a lingering smile at sleeping Fred and pattered off with them. And another summer's day was done.

4

Grumble Strikes Again

Summer had long gone. Now it was deep winter in the forest. The north wind blew. Robins chatted, shivered, and hid their heads under their wings. The poor things were cold. Snow lay all about, deep and crisp and even, and the Bottle Rabbit was stamping up and down outside Fred and Charlie's cabin, trying to keep his paws warm while waiting for Emily. Good old Charlie now looked out. He stood at the cabin door for a moment and quickly closed it again. The big Clydesdale had been shovelling snow early – his nose still looked red and raw – but he and Fred were spending the morning in armchairs on either side of a roaring fire of pine-logs, glancing through the *Forest Echo* and the *Gazette*, sipping mulled wine. Flakes of snow dropped down their chimney and sizzled on the logs. A roast of pork turned on a spit over the flames, smoking and crackling; Charlie was watching it carefully. Outside, the Bottle Rabbit had to keep skipping up and down to keep warm. He blew on his nails, and kept a sharp eye out for a band of snowballing young stoats who tended to overdo the fooling about in this sort of weather.

Up came Emily, white as the falling snow, pulling a sled behind her. 'There's skating on Big

Pond, Bottle Rabbit; let's go there.'

'Well – I'm no great hand at skating – but yes, let's,' and they set off through the woods, following down beside the stream that led to Big Pond. The forest brook itself was half frozen. Brown skeletons of leaves lay lagging its edges. In the wintry weather silent birds sat brooding on snow-laden branches of leafless trees.

But Big Pond, a fine lake that lay close underneath the mountain, was alive with young animals of all kinds in brilliant red, orange, yellow, green, blue, indigo and violet woolly caps, whooping and whistling and shouting and laughing as their skates hissed along the polished ice. Nearly all the huge pond had been cleared of snow and the skaters were everywhere. Their voices echoed and re-echoed through the forest, and every icy crag tinkled like iron.

Emily was a fine skater, and soon her elegant white cat-body was swooping and swerving through the throng. The Bottle Rabbit was more of a bumbling kind of skater, but he trod boldly out and managed to trundle around contentedly, though sometimes sitting down with a bump. 'How do those cats manage it?' he wondered aloud, when a long line of Tiger Toms went hurtling by. They seemed to twist and turn like one enormous, linked cat as they racketed away across the ice.

Emily, now leaving the tumultuous throng, went twirling and swooping and dancing off by herself across the lake, a trim, white, exquisite little figure with her tail looped up in one front paw. She ranged far across the lake but always came back to the Bottle Rabbit. And so they skated all morning long.

At noon some small brown bears lit braziers near the lake shore and all the animals crowded round the glowing charcoal to warm their chilled paws. The bears heated up cocoa in black cooking pots and handed it out to everyone in china mugs. Then a great cheer went up as the Golden Baker appeared, pushing his three-wheeled delivery cart with a load of hot steaming pies in it. There was some cheerful scuffling among the young tom-cats and stoats for the pies, but a few words from the Golden Baker soon established order, and everyone happily gulped and munched.

'Now, let's take the sled right across the lake, Emily.'

'What a very good idea.'

So the Bottle Rabbit climbed on in front and Emily with a few strokes of her skates got the sled up to a high speed, leapt on behind him and crouched with her front paws on his shoulders. Cat and rabbit went whistling across the crackling ice. A pale sun behind them lit up the snow-caked pine trees and the lake itself. As they sped across they could faintly see an image of themselves in another sled in the gleaming bosom of the lake.

At the far side, uncleared snow gently bumped them to a halt. 'Wasn't that terrific?' said the Bottle Rabbit.

'Lovely,' said Emily, 'let's do the same thing back.'

'Yes, but we've never been over here before; let's take a quick look in the forest first.'

So they undid their skates with hurried, numbed paws, threw them clanking into the sled, and scrambled and stumbled off into a dark forest light with snow-whiteness. They started chasing one another and snowballing one another and playing a sort of two-animal hide-and-seek with one another. Emily kept winning because she had the sense to follow the Bottle Rabbit's paw-marks, whereas he just went rushing towards where he was sure she was. Then the fourth time they did it the Bottle Rabbit finally caught Emily behind a clump of low-branched alders. Just as he was gasping 'Ally ally in free' and putting his paws over her eyes, a strange voice spoke and a shadow hung over them.

'Well, well, well; hello, hello. I do believe we've met before, haven't we? Too delightful to meet again like this.'

It was a cracked, husky, but also plummy, ladylike voice. They looked up and saw an extraordinary great creature standing over them, a colossal haystacky heap of a shapeless kind of Thing, with straws sticking out everywhere. The Thing was covered with snow as well, and it looked like a huge partly-nibbled ferocious coconut bun. There was a ladylike smile on its battered face, though. The Bottle Rabbit and Emily, who had been laughing hard, suddenly went silent. Their hearts sank for they knew that this was the Mother of that horrible monster the Grumble, and they remembered the trick they'd played on her once before. What was she going to say to them, or do to them now?

'Having a very jolly time in the snow, are we? Well, well. Animals will be animals. But how nice to see you again. Such nice friendly helpful little creatures you were when you first came to see us. Such a pity you had to leave so early. *So* kind about trying to find me my port when I'd lost my specs. That dratted Merritt again, of course. What

61

my Grumb' sees in him I'm simply unable to understand. It can't be his singing, surely? Well, you must come along with me and have a nice glass of, or rather a nice cup of tea. It's tea-time, you know. And I can't persuade my boy to take it anymore. Nothing but dark rum will do for him, he says. And I don't suppose that absurd Merritt would know how to hold a cup and saucer if you told him to. So do come along. It's really not far to our winter palace. Under the sea, you know. *So* convenient.' She peered down short-sightedly. Then she grabbed each of them in one of her powerful claw-like hands. Close up she was as heavy and hairy and smelly as ever.

'But we have to get back to our friends,' the animals said with one voice. It was a relief, of course, that the Grumble's Mother had not grasped that they had tricked her last time they met, but they were horrified at the idea of going anywhere near the frightening Grumble again *or* his ugly little associate, the Merritt.

'No. It's my tea-time. I must insist. I won't take no for an answer. I must have company at tea-time.' And the grotesque haystacky creature literally dragged the two poor animals off with her through the snow.

The night grew darker now and the wind blew colder as the Grumble's Mother took them on a long journey away from the lake and the skaters, away from their friends, out of the forest, over the wolf slopes, the windy headlands, down to the secret land, out into the surging waves. She grasped them close and again made that dreadful heart-cold plunge, this time to the Grumble's sea home, his echoing under-ocean den, sealed at the entrance with an enormous stone.

As the great imprisoning stone door swung closed behind them with a crash, the Bottle Rabbit and Emily, shivering with cold and apprehension, saw an even vaster and darker hall than the one under Grumble Lake that the monster had once taken them to by force. At one end of this sea-den a huge fire roared and crackled, and they could see the Grumble and the Merritt; they were sitting there at a long table in front of the flames, casting jagged shadows down towards the three new-comers. The Grumble was mounted on a sort of

63

crude wooden throne and the scrawny little Merritt was perched on a heap of books piled on a camp-stool. Neither looked up. Both were devouring fish, shiny-scaled fish from a barrel that they impaled on what looked like whale tusks and then toasted whole in the flames. The huge, hairy, evil-smelling Grumble had a dishevelled pile of fishy bones lying around him nearly up to his great knees. The careful Merritt had a neat heap arranged in rows beside him, each fish's backbone picked as clean as a whistle, each fish head still attached, its fish eyes staring out into the hall. Both creatures sucked and chewed in a revoltingly noisy way, and took swigs of dark rum between bites of fish.

The Merritt, who had an ancient volume open on his knee, was talking in his scratchy voice.

'Here's another good riddle, Grumble. It's Old English again. They're the best, you know. See what you can do with this one. It's pretty good. Really quite amusing.' He sniggered. 'Here it is: "I saw a woman sitting alone."'

The Grumble munched fish and stared at him.

'What?'

'"I saw a woman sitting alone"?'

The Grumble swallowed his fish.

'Beats me.'

'Answer's Hen.'

'What?'

'*Hen*.'

The Grumble took another swig of rum and bit off a hunk of half-cooked cod.

'What do you mean, Hen? Don't be stupid.'

'Well, that's what it says here.'

'What a stupid game, Merritt. Forget the riddles. Listen: fill my pipes and bring me another big bowl of rum.'

The Merritt did all this and the Grumble gulped and puffed and munched and puffed and gulped, the Merritt crouching obsequiously nearby.

Then the Grumble noticed through bleary eyes the group standing at the door.

'You back already, Mum? Early, aren't you?' ('Thought we'd be having a bit of peace and quiet for once,' he said aside to the Merritt in a low voice that everybody could hear. 'No getting rid of her, is there?') 'And what on earth have you got *there*?' he suddenly roared, pointing with a half-eaten flounder at the sopping wet cat and rabbit.

His Mother smiled and nodded and nodded and smiled and pushed the Bottle Rabbit and Emily forward in front of her, smiling away. The Grumble at close quarters was looking as horrible as ever, hairy and huge and now gripping his whalebone with a whole haddock on it in one fist and his bowl of dark rum in the other.

'Some dear little friends of mine. I've invited them to afternoon tea. And they've been good enough to come.'

'Good afternoon – ' began Emily.

'We'll have 'em for breakfast tomorrow.'

The two young animals stepped back in alarm. The Merritt screeched delightedly.

'Don't worry, dears. It's only his fun,' said the Grumble's Mother. 'Such a tease, my little Grumb'. Don't take any notice.' She peered round. 'Now we'll all take a nice cup of tea. I like a cup of tea at this hour. Which do you prefer? Earl

65

Grey? Lapsang Souchong?' She started pottering about with cups.

'Thank goodness Count Hubert isn't here with us,' whispered Emily to the Bottle Rabbit. 'All this would have frightened the poor little animal out of his skin.'

'It's frightening *me* out of *my* skin,' whispered the Bottle Rabbit, and he couldn't help noticing that poor Emily's fur was standing up all over. But at least the place was lovely and warm and they both began to feel dry.

'Oh drat this teapot.' The Grumble's Mother banged a squat earthenware teapot down and took up her familiar cry: 'Where's me port?' She strode over to a very large keg set on a trestle, lifted it in her powerful arms, sniffed at it, then swallowed and swallowed, her thick pebbly-glassed spectacles gleaming in the firelight, her hairy lips smacking between gulps. 'Ha. That's better,' she grunted, and did the same thing again and again. At last she dropped the keg with a clatter. Then she lumped down heavily into a broken-backed armchair with its springs sticking out.

'Time for forty winks, I think, all things considered,' she muttered thickly. '*So* tiring, you know, sploshing about in the ocean waves. Sploshing about in the waves.' She raised her voice again: '*Do* make yourselves at home and for goodness sake don't just stand about. I can't *stand* people who just stand about and gawp. I won't have it. *So* ill-bred. So sit down on the sofa and my boy Grumble will entertain you, I'm sure. Go on, entertain 'em, Grumb'.' She yawned, and her voice grew thicker and thicker. 'I'm sure you'll find a great deal to talk about. You have *so* much in common. Wonderful weather we've been . . .' Her head lolled and she started to snore, her heavy haystacky body heaving and rumbling. Emily and the Bottle Rabbit sat down on the sofa gingerly.

The Grumble and the Merritt continued to ignore them and went on munching and gulping.

'Got another riddle for you, Grumble,' the Merritt suddenly said.

'Umph?'

'Here's another riddle. Listen to this: "Wonder was in the waves: water went to bone." '

The Grumble just stared in front of him with glazed eyes. Emily whispered to the Bottle Rabbit, 'You know, that's rather nice.' Then she said out loud, in a timid voice, '"Wonder was in the waves: water went to bone." Could it be an iceberg? I mean the waves get frozen and hard like a bone?'

'Not fair. Not fair,' screeched the Merritt. 'You looked. You looked at the answers in my book.'

'I – I didn't,' stammered Emily, but the Grumble was angry now, too.

'I knew it was iceberg all the time. I'm not a fool, you know. Water. Bone. Stands to reason it's iceberg.'

Then he squinted at the two animals more closely.

'*Wait* a minute. *You're* not friends of my Mum's. I know you two. I bagged you on Grumble Mere and brought you down to my den for dinner. Spiced rabbit stew I was going to make. Yes. And sliced cat for breakfast. Then you opened the door and let the wet in while I was having my little nap.'

'Right, Grumb',' screeched the Merritt, 'and they got me wet, too; wet my best suit. They're very bad. Very very very very bad. You should eat 'em up soon.'

'Oh shut up about your suit, Merritt. And don't call me Grumb'. But I'll eat 'em up all right.' He downed another bowl of rum and finished off most of the great lump of whiting on his whalebone. 'Trouble is, I've had so much fish. Hundreds of fish. Cod, plaice, bass, flounder, bluefish, mackerel, herring, tuna, whiting, sardines even.' His eyes went glazed again. 'I'm full.'

'We could lock them in the pantry till tomorrow,' said the Merritt. 'Serve 'em right, barging in here like that.'

This was too much for the Bottle Rabbit. 'We certainly didn't come barging in here, did we, Emily?' Emily shook her head. 'The Grumble's Mother *made* us come,' he went on. 'We *hate* it here. It's ugly and dark and smelly and . . .' Emily put a calming white paw on his shoulder, but it was too late. The Grumble gave a great over-fed roar of anger and the Merritt skipped about in fury. (Emily noticed that he was wearing little black patent-leather half-boots.)

'Too much fish. I'm stuffed. I can't move,' bellowed the Grumble in his anger. 'Lucky for you –' He flailed about. 'But shove 'em in the pantry, Merritt. Quick. We'll fry 'em up for breakfast in the morning. With tomatoes and mushrooms.'

The Merritt leapt up, gleefully giggling and

scratching, and hustled the two poor animals over to a little door. He flung it open and thrust them into a long narrow room full of sacks and cans and barrels. The door slammed shut. Again they were prisoners.

They stood there for a while.

'At least we are on our own,' said Emily, at last.

'I can't stand that sneery little Merritt,' said the Bottle Rabbit.

They could hear thumpings and gruntings in the hall, and guessed that the Grumble and the Merritt were finishing off their barrel of rum, because soon two more lots of snorings could be heard. Otherwise all was silence, save the distant pounding of water on the walls of the Grumble's deep-sea home.

The situation certainly looked bleak for the two animals, locked away in a pantry at the bottom of the sea, late at night, far from their friends, no bedding, and with a ravening drunkard of a monster eager to fry them up for breakfast. But they did not give up hope.

'Let's think this thing out calmly,' said Emily.

'*Calmly*? Oh well, all right, I'll try.'

'I can't think of anything I can do,' said Emily, 'but there *is* your Magic Bottle. All right,' she lifted a gentle paw as the Bottle Rabbit seemed to be raising a hot-headed objection. 'We know the Blue Hares can't fly here; we know the Golden Eagle can't fly here; and anyway he needs help when he's over water; and obviously the Twelve Mice can't get here either with their coach. But we can get sandwiches and drinks, probably, if that business works underwater. Not that I'm in the

least hungry, after watching the Grumble gol-
loping his fish down like that.'

'Well, I *am* hungry,' said the Bottle Rabbit. 'And
I'm going to try a pongle. Yes, I'll do a pongle.
Perhaps we could build up a great bank of ham
sandwiches and sort of sneak past them while
they're eating them?' He was getting desperate.

'Mm. Yes. But wouldn't the Grumble swallow
any number of sandwiches in about one minute
flat?' said Emily. 'And anyhow don't you think it
sounds a bit ridiculous? And also how could we
open that massive front door, push that huge
stone away?'

'No, we can't,' said the rabbit hopelessly.

'Look,' said Emily, 'how about if you pongled
up the Mice? They'd come to the seashore, stop –
and – and – well, perhaps they'd think of
something.'

The Bottle Rabbit looked at her sombrely. He
could see she was near the end of her tether, too.
'May as well give it a go.' So he hunched his
shoulders with a sad face and pongled five times:
'Pongle . . . Pongle . . . Pongle . . . Pongle . . . Pongle.' He looked at Emily again. 'After all, the
Bottle's done marvellous things for us in the past.
Perhaps they'll be out there soon.' He smiled
painfully, braced his bowed shoulders, and now
pongled up a moody sandwich. A long night was
ahead of them.

Had they only known it, their friends were
already at work. It was not long after this that the
Twelve Mice came jingling up, with cheerful cries,
to that grey point on the seashore where the

Grumble's Mother had plunged into the waves. It had snowed heavily again, so the powerful-bodied Mice had arrived not with the state carriage but with an elegant covered sleigh, alive with bells and charmingly decorated. But their bells and greetings soon died away in the snow.

'Something's wrong here,' said Nigel, the courier-mouse who carried the post-horn. 'They're in trouble. They've been taken. And look at those tracks leading straight into the water. What's been going on?' Sure enough, there were slurry marks showing the Grumble's Mother's passage. Nigel stood in thought for some time. 'If only Norman were here,' he said at last. 'Norman knows every seagull on the coast. They're the chaps we need.'

The group of Twelve Mice stood in the snow, puzzled about what to do next. 'Why not get the

71

Golden Eagle to find him?' put in a bright young red-haired mouse.

'Good thinking, Curtis,' said Nigel. 'I'll do precisely that.' And straight away he blew the Golden Eagle notes on his post-horn.

Within minutes that astonishing bird was at his side and Nigel was pouring out his story. 'Norman last seen in Naples,' said the Golden Eagle. 'Wait here. Back soon.' The Golden Eagle of course could fly at extraordinary speeds and could see a thousand miles in any direction from high up.

All the Mice could do now was wait. They walked up and down. They drank hot tea from thermoses to keep out the intense cold. They stared up at the thick white sky. Some of them tried to get a game of cards going under the sleigh's fringed canopy. But no one had the heart for it. Too much worry about their friends, the Bottle Rabbit and Emily, was in the air.

At last came that tearing rushing crackle of the Golden Eagle's great wings again, high in the sky. Down he swooped beside Nigel, his magnificent head held high, his golden breast panting, and all in one breath he said: 'Norman says sorry he's busy he can't come says Hi to everybody especially Nigel and that terrific Bottle Rabbit says Naples is great and full of naughty boys and so was Venice says get in touch with the Wampiti* Gulls as quick as poss I'm going to get them now.'

And with a flash of his wings the Golden Eagle had raced back up into the sky. They lost sight of

* Pronounced WOM-pee-tee.

him up in the crumbling woolly fast-dropping snow but knew he'd soon find the Wampitis. 'Let's hope they're not far off,' Nigel said to a quiet fellow-mouse, who nodded patiently.

The Wampitis weren't far off as it turned out. The Mice all heard a rush and flutter of many wings, a high harsh calling of seagulls' voices and the answering deep notes of the Golden Eagle; then that great Messenger came swooping back to Nigel. 'Wampiti Gulls say this is Grumble's sea-den say it's well-nigh impregnable say maybe Sam the Bear say they'll mark the spot for Sam the Bear I'm getting him now.' And off he flew.

Meanwhile, down in the Grumble's sea-den the hours were moving slowly but surely towards breakfast-time. The two young animals sat glumly side by side in the pantry, trying not to listen to the harsh chorus of the snoring three.

They talked, to cheer themselves up: 'Anyway it was lovely skating, wasn't it, Emily?'

'Yes, I had a wonderful time. And the sledding too. And the pies and cocoa. And you know what? I think something's going to work out. I feel it in my catbones.'

The Bottle Rabbit gulped and reached for her paw.

On the seashore the Mice were now stamping about in the falling snow and flapping their front paws under their armpits, trying to keep warm. They talked in low voices. 'Got any cheese, Bill?' 'What's a Grumble?' 'How tall is Sam the Bear?' 'There's snow in my wellingtons.' 'That Norman's a caution.' 'Bitter weather, this.' 'Conrad was late again.' 'I could do with a ginger beer.' 'I could do with a real beer.' 'Straighten your tie, Geoffrey, they may be here any minute.' The usual Mouse-talk. But they were all uneasy and impatient.

The fresh snow was now so thick on the ground that the Mice didn't notice Sam's characteristic thudding approach, and he was almost upon them when they first heard his heavy Scrunch, Pause. Scrunch, Pause. The great bear was hurtling to the rescue through the white night. Nothing could stop him, and a hearty cheer arose when he hove in sight, his mighty chest streaked with snow, his great head white with heavy flakes.

'Oh Sam, Sam, thank goodness you've come,' cried Nigel, and the young red-haired mouse, Curtis, skipped up and down.

Sam just grunted, 'Where?' and the Golden Eagle was at his side in an instant, pointing through the swirling snow out to sea.

There, dimly discernible, a great flock of sea-gulls was diving and fluttering low over the water, rising and falling, changing and inter-changing, but always staying in the same heaving dark place. 'Those the Wampitis?' asked Sam, curtly. The Golden Eagle nodded his high, visionary, beaked head in assent, and then, pausing only to don a pair of heavy-duty black-and-yellow striped knee-length trunks, Sam the Bear, whose splendid hairy body could withstand even Arctic weather conditions, plunged into the icy foam and sank down to the bottom of the sea.

*

In his den the Grumble was twitching and groaning. He was beginning to wake up. He stretched a gross arm out, feeling for and finding a bowl of rum, then staggered to his feet and launched a clumsy kick at the Merritt, who was lying curled and abject on the floor. At that moment there came a thunderous clash and rumble, and to his drop-jawed astonishment the Grumble saw the massive stone door of his hall begin to shake and then to move.

'Hey, watch it! Stop that!' he bawled. 'What's going on?' Still not fully awake he turned with a snarl and grabbed up a great saw-toothed whaling knife. When he swung back he gasped in amazement. Standing in the open doorway with sea water pouring from his yellow-and-black trunks was the towering figure of Sam the Bear, black and huge, his great dark eyes fixed on the Grumble's, his whole body rigid with honest fury.

The Grumble curled his hideous upper lip. 'Out of my den, Bear. Take that!' he bellowed, and made to throw the whaling knife straight at Sam's heart. But Sam, with one heavy bound, was on him. The Grumble could do nothing. With a twist of his muscular arm Sam had the knife out of the Grumble's claw-like hand and then, with his free paw, he cuffed and cuffed and cuffed the rum-sodden brute. The Grumble yelled and yelled, but Sam was really angry, and his last cuff actually knocked the Grumble out. The vile creature tumbled to the ground, where he was to lie supine for a long time.

Now the only sounds to be heard were the stertorous grunts of the still-snoring Mother. Sam slowly shrugged his great shoulders, looked round, picked up the barrel of rum and ambled over to where the Merritt had been crouching in silent fear. 'It wasn't me! It wasn't me! I haven't done anything! Leave me alone! I wasn't going to eat them for breakfast! I don't like rabbit! Leave me alone!' he gabbled in cowardly surrender.

So Sam picked the Merritt up by the feet and dumped him headfirst into the rum barrel. How the Merritt kicked and screeched! So Sam pulled him out again, and with another shrug he dumped him on the sofa. The Merritt cowered there. Then something made the bear seize the barrel of thick dark sticky rum, up-end it, and pour the rest of it all over the prostrate Grumble. The Grumble stirred and seemed to make scooping motions with his hands, then fell back. 'What a set,' murmured Sam, who was now quite calm. 'How well the poet has it:

> Thou Demon Drink, thou fell Destroyer
> Society's curse, and its greatest Annoyer.'

The Merritt still crouched, sticky, in a corner. 'It's my best suit. You've utterly ruined my best suit,' he whined.

Sam pointed a great paw at him. 'Silence,' he boomed. 'Now listen to me, Merritt. Tell your friend Grumble when he comes to –' ('He's not my friend, he never was my friend,' yelped the Merritt cravenly) – 'tell your friend, miserable turncoat that you are, that if you ever, any of you, set foot in the forest again I shall be back to deal with you in terrible ways. I mean that – in terrible

ways. I think he'll understand.' Sam chose simply
to ignore the besotted old snorer in the corner.
'Now show me where my friends are and get out
of my sight forever.' The rum-soaked Merritt
pointed with a shaking finger at the pantry door.
Ignoring the proffered key, Sam strode over and
stove the door in with one mighty blow. The
Bottle Rabbit and Emily, who had been listening
to all this with hearts aglow, leapt into his arms.

'Here, take these heavy fisherman's knitted
sweaters and we'll go,' said Sam gently. They put
on the two sweaters he had produced from a
watertight plastic bag. 'Now jump on my back,
hold on tight, and we'll be there before you know
it.' He strode to the edge of the hall, shoved back
the door and leapt out into the sea. The last sight
of the den that they had was of an outstretched,
rum-covered Grumble, a snoring Mother, and a
Merritt weakly mopping and mowing and licking
rum off his hands.

Moving at high speed, Sam the Bear reached
the shore in minutes. The rejoicing Mice, who had
been busy gathering winter fuel, now had a fine
bonfire of driftwood going against the blood-
freezing cold, and Emily and the Bottle Rabbit
pulled off their dripping sweaters, wrapped
themselves in warm blankets supplied by Nigel,
and gratefully drank down the tea laced with
brandy that the prudent mouse had ready for
them. Sam decided to carry them straight home
himself, so very soon they waved goodbye to the
loyal mice and thanked them. 'And our best to the
Wampitis,' called the Bottle Rabbit. Then they
were off in the morning light, with Sam pounding

back home through the forest.

In no time at all they were at Fred and Charlie's cabin. The fire still burned brightly, the kettle bubbled on the hob. Breakfast was ready. Fred and Charlie both beamed and beamed as they moved about, serving hot porridge and bacon and eggs, and a pot of strong tea. The two animals ate heartily.

'A rum creature, that Grumble,' remarked Fred to Charlie, 'very rum.'

'Yes, and the Merritt likes it a lot too,' put in the Bottle Rabbit.

Charlie smiled and patted him on the head. The Bottle Rabbit finished off his last piece of hot buttered toast. 'Ah, that *was* good,' he said, yawning and stretching his long floppy ears. 'We'll have a little snooze now.' He glanced out into the woods, where the snow lay dinted with stoat-paws. 'There's more snow, more and more snow falling. Perhaps we'll go sledding again this afternoon . . .' He fell asleep as he spoke. Emily was quiet beside him. Sam the Bear and Fred and Charlie were peacefully drinking tea round the fire. In the forest the north wind still blew, and the snow fell and fell. But in the warm cabin cat and rabbit slept safe and sound.

5

Bottle Rabbit Speaks French

It was spring again, so one day the Bottle Rabbit thought he'd try doing some French. He was sitting outside Fred and Charlie's cabin in the early morning sunshine with his glass of milk and his bun, looking up at the clear blue sky.

'*Marcel a sa plume, Denise a son crayon*,'* he said out loud to himself, quietly, at the same time shrugging his shoulders, raising his eyebrows and spreading his paws. Then, having another go, '*Le soleil brillait dans un ciel clair*.'† More shrugging and paw-spreading.

A light shadow passed in front of him.

'Bottle Rabbit, what on earth are you doing?' Emily had softly arrived.

'Nothing special. Why?'

'Well, your face was, well, it was like a soft balloon, sort of crinkly, when some of the air has come out.'

'Oh, really?'

At this point up loped a big black cat with a thick moustache. He wore a black cape and a wide-brimmed black hat and he swayed as he walked.

---

* Marcel has his pen, Denise has her pencil.
† The sun was shining in a clear sky.

'Good morning, monsieur. And a very good morning to you, mademoiselle.' He was a real French cat, it seemed. He bowed and smiled at Emily as he loped on. When he smiled his moustache went up under his nose, and his nose came down over his moustache.

'What a striking-looking cat,' said Emily, glancing sideways after him.

'I didn't think he was all that special,' said the Bottle Rabbit, who now definitely didn't want to do any more French. 'Why's he wearing that silly cloak, for instance? I tell you what, let's go down to the woods and see the Golden Baker. I wouldn't mind one of his big sausage-rolls and some lemonade.'

'Sausage-rolls? Really? At this time of day?' said Emily. 'Surely *croissants* would be more the thing?'

'What's wrong with good old sausage-rolls?'

80

Emily shrugged, smiled, and put out a friendly paw. The Bottle Rabbit took it in his and together they ambled off into the forest.

The Golden Baker was sitting on his tricycle in a sunny glade, surrounded by cheerful squirrels and some small bears. As the Bottle Rabbit had hoped, he had lovely big sensible sausage-rolls and cold fresh lemonade in an earthenware jar. Happy animals stood about, munching and gulping and chatting.

'There's a big black cat looking for you,' said the Golden Baker to Emily. 'Foreigner by the look of him. Wasn't half interested in finding you.' He winked at the Bottle Rabbit.

Now a high tenor voice echoed in the trees: '*Parlez-moi d'amour*,'* it sang. Then came a whiff of scent and the French cat sprang into view, white teeth flashing through the forest shadows.

'*Bonjour, chère m'selle*,'† he said to Emily in his throaty way. 'Permit me to present myself. I am called Raoul.' And with that he swept Emily's delicate paw up in his long thin one and implanted a kiss.

'How do you do?' said Emily.

'What pleasure this gives me to meet you again one time.' Raoul swung his cape round his shoulders. 'Oh, by hazard, are you free this evening?'

'Yes – er, yes, I believe I am,' said Emily, turning quite pink over her whole white cat-body.

'But what about the Animals' Spring Charity

* Speak to me of love.
† Good morning, my dear young lady.

Ball – ?' began the Bottle Rabbit.

'But it is perfect,' interrupted Raoul, smiling so that his moustache went up under his nose, and his nose came down over his moustache. 'Now I tell you what 'appens. I come from 'elping with, how-you-say, Spring Bal. I fix everything. During big dancing and eating we 'ave also Raffle you know.'

The squirrels and small bears exclaimed excitedly.

'You know what it is a Raffle,' went on Raoul. 'Everybodies buy ticket. Then there is big Draw. And Big Prizes. And then also much monies to help some poor blokes.'

Of course, all the forest knew about Raffles. Pob was a great Raffle-person. 'All come here,' he would say, 'I sell you ticket. Some time you win, some time no. But always nice money for old animals, poor animals.' Pob did this a lot and was very good and careful about it and made sure old and poor animals got all the money. But Pob was off at the seaside with an aunt for a week, and somehow Raoul, this stranger, had taken over the Raffle.

'Very well,' he now said, 'everybodies bring some coins to the Bal and we dance and eat and drink and have Raffle. Especial *we* dance,' he added, gazing at Emily.

The squirrels and small bears cheered, Emily looked bashful and pleased, the Golden Baker grinned, and the Bottle Rabbit munched on his sausage-roll. Raoul took his leave, sauntering off into the forest.

*

Late that evening the trees around the cricket pavilion were hung with bright-coloured lanterns that blinked and twinkled in the warm summer dark. Already many animals were laughing and chatting there. When the Bottle Rabbit arrived, Fred and Charlie, Count Hubert, the Golden Baker, Norman the Pigeon (tonight sporting an orange silk shirt over designer jeans), Emily herself, and a host of other forest friends were milling around. Sam's wife, Maud the Bear, was there, and so were the Golden Baker's three sisters and Charlie's cousin Alma, but Fred's friend, Daisy the armadillo, hadn't been able to get away from circus duties. A band was playing on a raised platform. Booge People had come down from their hills for this Ball with their wheeled instruments. There they were, small and hairy and

happy, as they blew and plucked and beat on bassoons, basset horns, bagpipes, bass fiddles, bass drums, bongos and bones. All their instruments (except the bones) were on wheels, biggish, pram-sized wheels. Tonight they were playing wonderfully bouncy, get-up-and-dancey jigs and polkas, with occasional waltzes. Sometimes three especially hairy Booge People stood in front and sang in close harmony.

But the high tenor voice of Raoul could be heard over everything else – organizing the Raffle. Animals were queuing up in dozens to buy Raffle tickets and the money-bag on the Raffle table grew fatter and heavier every minute.

'Rather a noisy sort of fellow, isn't he?' said Sam the Bear to Maud. 'But there, it's all rather different abroad, I expect. They're more excitable. The hotter weather, you know. Perfectly understandable thing.'

Crowds of animals were dancing vigorously. The Bottle Rabbit was just plucking up courage to invite Emily when, 'You like perhaps I dance with you, m'selle, no? But yes of course you will like to.' It was Raoul, who swept Emily off, his nose and moustache rising and falling, his long black tail beating the rhythm as his supple body leapt and plunged, bearing Emily with him. Emily dipped and swayed in perfect time with Raoul. A little crowd formed around them, rapt in admiration and exultation at their skill.

The Bottle Rabbit sat alone. All his friends – Fred, Charlie, Sam – all of them – were skipping about happily, enjoying themselves – and he felt out of it. He loved leaping about to music, but he'd never been much good at ballroom dancing, could only just manage a slow waltz by counting carefully. Glumly he sipped his lemonade.

The Booge People had stopped for a breather, and Emily, flushed and excited, slid down next to the Bottle Rabbit. 'Do come and try the next one. You'll love it. They play so well. The tunes . . . the rhythms . . .'

'Mm,' said the Bottle Rabbit.

More and more animals kept arriving, including a busload of Tiger Toms and their Tabbies, all gorgeously turned out, great dancers all. Also some distinguished-looking foreign cats.

'Why,' said Emily, 'there's Philippe and Josette; they must be over from Paris. What a coincidence! I really must introduce them to Raoul.'

But the music was starting again, and now there was no escape for the Bottle Rabbit. 'Come on, have a go!' all his friends chorused. Raoul had pranced off – 'It is now soon the Raffle-time' – and Emily at last led the Bottle Rabbit out to dance. The Booge People had swung into a samba, and it was a bit of a disaster for him. He couldn't keep time, he tripped over his own paws, he stood on Emily's. The music was too loud, it went on too long, and he knew the other animals were laughing at him, even his friends. Then came a tap on his shoulder. 'You excuse me, *hein*?' It was Raoul, who swept Emily off yet again with a graceful twirl of his tail. Emily smiled apologetically over his shoulder and the Bottle Rabbit stood there, his taut woolly body filled with sadness. Back he crept to his table and sat down, totally fed up.

And things got even worse. When Emily at last

came back again, hot and flushed, saying, 'Bottle Rabbit, I'm dying of thirst,' he went and got two brimming glasses of herb beer from the bar. 'Lovely,' said Emily, then, 'Oh, oh no!' as the herb beer spilled all over her. 'Oh, Bottle Rabbit, do be careful!'

The miserable rabbit had somehow lost his balance. Had he been pushed? Over his shoulder he saw a black-caped figure slipping away through the cheerful throng.

'Never mind, Bottle Rabbit, I'll soon be dry,' said Emily, mopping and squeezing away and keeping a fairly cheerful face. 'Isn't the music heavenly?'

The Bottle Rabbit just sat there.

Then came the Raffle.

'Animals! Animals all! May I have your attention?' called a commanding voice. It was Sam the Bear again.

'Animals! It is now Raffle time and, yes, I shall now award the prizes.' He put on an enormous pair of spectacles.

All the animals crowded around the Raffle tables as little Count Hubert excitedly pulled out the winning numbers from the barrel.

'Ah ha!' said Sam, looking over his spectacles. 'Yes. The First Prize, a three-speed bicycle, goes to Harry.' Amidst loud applause Harry, an eager young Tiger Tom, happily picked up his new bike. 'A very fine machine,' said Sam the Bear.

'The Second Prize. Let me see. What have we here? Ah, yes. Yes. A complete set of the *Animals' Encyclopaedia* bound in green leatherette. Capital. Capital.' This prize went to a quiet studious vole.

And the great Clydesdale, Fred, was pleased to accept the Third Prize, a case of assorted home-made jams and marmalades. 'Just the thing for Sunday breakfasts,' he said to Charlie. Charlie nodded and smiled.

And then there was one more prize, the Booby Prize, added as a joke.

'Also,' said Sam the Bear in a loud voice, 'yes, also it is my pleasant duty to award the Booby Prize, all in the greatest fun, need I say. It goes this year, let me see, yes, it goes this year to our dear good forest friend – the Bottle Rabbit!' There was much laughter and some clapping as the embarrassed animal pushed up to the front to collect his prize – a small inflatable rubber duck.

'Just the thing for your Saturday Night Barf!' shouted a weasel in a cloth cap. Animals laughed. The Bottle Rabbit wearily found his seat and sat there, his ears down, clutching the limp duck, wishing he could go home.

But dancing had begun again. After a while the Booge People started up one of their specials, a short, sharp number. Bongo- and bones-players began a clattering set of rhythms and soon bassoons and bagpipes were hooting out a strange stabbing tune against this throbbing beat. By now the crowd was on its feet, hopping up and down as the harsh music grew wilder and wilder. Even the Bottle Rabbit's back paws were thumping under the table. Then the string-basses joined in with a whirling roar that grew louder still until suddenly with a CRASH it all ended as quickly as it had begun. The silence now was broken only by the soft pad-pad of the studious vole, caught up in his own dance, eyes closed, his mind on plashy fens, whispering to himself, a paw gripping Volume One of the *Animals' Encyclopaedia*. Then more loud applause came for the hairy Booge People as they put aside their wheeled instruments and bowed and flexed their paws. It was time for another breather.

The Bottle Rabbit had cheered up quite a lot and had even started blowing up his duck, encouraged by Norman, who had also told him what he thought of Raoul. 'Well, frankly, I think he's a bit much. I mean, that *absurd* cape, those *showy* pirouettes, and especially that *huge* black bottom of his. Well, he simply hasn't got the figure for it, has he, lovey?' He smiled at the Bottle Rabbit, who was liking him more and more. The rabbit's duck took shape; it had a big beak.

Meanwhile Emily, still a little damp, was talking to her Parisian cat-friends, who spoke courteously to the Bottle Rabbit. 'That's a good duck you have, isn't it?' said Philippe, whose English was quite good. 'Oh,' said Emily, 'that reminds me. I must introduce you to a fellow country-cat of yours, Raoul, the one who's doing the Grand Raffle. But

– where *is* Raoul – where has he gone?'

In truth Raoul was nowhere to be seen. What's more, there was a commotion at the Raffle table. Sam the Bear was looking concerned. Other animals were calling to one another and searching – on the ground, under the table, in the neighbouring trees.

'Where is it? Where's it gone? Saw it just a minute ago. Where's the Raffle bag?' All talk broke off when Sam clapped his huge paws together for silence.

'Uh – oh,' whispered Norman. 'Something's up. I knew it. I knew it.'

'May I have your attention, friends,' called Sam. 'I'm the Bearer – ahem – I'm the bearer of unfortunate news. Yes, somehow the bag has been mislaid. The bag containing the Raffle money destined for old and poor animals' – a gasp from the crowd ' – Moreover, I very much fear that one in our midst is responsible. That one is none other than our French visitor, the cat, Raymond!'

'You mean Raoul, don't you?' said the Golden Baker.

'Yes, yes, yes, of course – whatever his outlandish name may be – this – Raoul – as you call him – seems to be the miscreant in question . . .'

But Sam's voice was for once lost in the great hubbub – a hubbub dominated by the harsh cries of Tiger Toms angered at this blow to their cat-pride. Even Emily looked flushed and annoyed, as she tried to explain it all to her puzzled French friends. 'So it is in effect a *Grand Rafle*?'* said Philippe.

* Big theft.

89

By now the Tiger Toms, bristling, had formed a line, as was their habit when working together: 'Get-that-cat, Get-that-bag! Get-that-cat, Get-that-bag!' they chanted hoarsely. They weaved about. 'Get-that-cat, Get-that-BAG!' Then with panthers' leaps they raced off into the forest, as their Tabbies nodded to one another with grim and approving smiles.

'I'm going too,' said the Bottle Rabbit. And before anyone could stop him he'd hopped off. He felt sure inside himself that he could thwart that Raoul.

Never had the forest seemed so dark to him. And it was full of frightening noises. Owls screeched and bats squeaked. A fox howled, a nameless creature screamed. The trees themselves creaked and scratched. The Bottle Rabbit shivered, and wished Emily was with him. Menacing shapes moved in the bushes as he hopped on. Distant whoops and yells echoed as the Tiger Toms called urgently to one another. But they were far away and he felt terribly alone.

Then, stumbling into a moonlit clearing, he suddenly heard *low breathings*. He stopped dead. And a large cat leapt out of the shadows and thrust a rapier at his chest. *'En garde!'** Raoul was on him. The sword didn't actually hurt much but the Bottle Rabbit gasped with the shock and his heart thumped.

'So it's you, Rabbit! It *would* be you. Well, I'm leaving. So just push off, Rabbit, you're not

* On guard.

wanted – I mean – Go from me, flee the camp, imbecile!' Raoul lifted up the heavy stolen Raffle bag he held in one paw and gave the Rabbit another nasty jab with his sword.

'Ow,' said the Bottle Rabbit, flinching away; and then he thought, 'What if he jabs again and cracks my Magic Bottle?' As though he had read his thoughts, Raoul now said, throatily, 'Also I take your Bottle with me, isn't it?' At this point the shocked rabbit had one of his really good ideas.

He stared hard over Raoul's right shoulder, and, his voice cracking, shouted, 'Fergus! Norman! At last! Help!'

91

Raoul, hesitating, looked over his shoulder. There was no one there, of course, but the Bottle Rabbit now had time to flip the sword aside and butt Raoul as hard as he could in his ample stomach. The big cat, with an 'Oomphh...', dropped the Raffle bag and collapsed on the ground gasping for breath.

The rabbit stared down at him, his heart beating faster than ever. 'Now what?' he asked himself. Raoul was already struggling up, wheezing and wheezing, reaching for his sword, scowling horribly.

Then to the Bottle Rabbit's amazement and relief, with a crash and a yell, a bevy of tough Tiger Toms burst through the undergrowth, Fergus in the lead, with Norman fluttering in the background.

Crash! Bash!! 'Ouch!' and in a moment Raoul was down on the ground again with four Tiger Toms sitting on him.

'Good man, Bottle Rabbit! We thought he'd given us the slip. Then we heard your shout.' Fergus, panting, glared at Raoul. 'Would you look at him. Isn't he a disgrace to all cat-hood?'

'Lemme go! Gerroff! That's my bad shoulder!' whined Raoul.

'Well, well, *well*,' it was Norman. 'You're not sounding very French to me *now*, I *must* say.'

'Course I'm not, stupid oaf. I'm no more French than you are,' gasped Raoul.

'That's right,' piped up a small voice from further back in the trees. It was a stoat named Francis. 'He's Vincent, he is. I'd know him anywhere. Used to sell fancy shirts in a shop in

Bilston. Not French at all.'

'*Bilston* – well, I *ask* you.' Norman tossed his head.

'All that's all very well,' said Fergus grimly. 'We've caught your man red-handed – all credit to you, Bottle Rabbit – and now he needs a lesson. A short, sharp one.' All the other Tiger Toms growled agreement. Raoul, or rather Vincent, looked alarmed.

'Give him a cat-drubbing!' shouted one of the tougher Tiger Toms.

'Right! Put in the cat-boot! Show him what's what!' shouted cat after cat. They ringed round the 'French' cat, paws clenched, muscles twitching. 'Knock him about! Let's go!' Vincent cowered away.

Then, 'One moment please; please wait just one moment. I'm a cat too, you know, and proud of it, but I don't like this rough justice.' It was Emily, who'd bounded gracefully up and now stood there outlined against a dark beech tree, flushed and bright-eyed. 'I see we have the Raffle bag back, thanks mostly to our dear Bottle Rabbit' – she smiled at him – 'so let us for goodness sake allow this wretched creature to depart. Let us not forget our basic cat-principles in the heat of the moment. Let us not descend to Raoul's, or rather Vincent's, un-cat-like level!'

A low growl of protest rose among some Tiger Toms, but she quickly quelled it with a glance. Emily was much respected in the cat world. Fergus, with a dry look, simply picked up the offender by the scruff of the neck, saying curtly, 'Very well. Think yourself lucky. But before you go, what have you to say for yourself at all? What kind of a gombeen cat is it would take money from old and poor animals?'

Vincent looked sulky. 'Well, in the first place it's not really a sword, just a piece of stick. Look. It's got a rubber end on it. Wouldn't hurt a fly. It was all just a bit of a joke, really. From a child I've always liked dressing up and acting and . . .'

'A joke, is it?' Fergus let Vincent drop to the ground with a thud. 'Was it any sort of a joke for the Bottle Rabbit out there in the dark like that?'

'Oh, come on. Don't be daft. I just did it for laughs. That nose-moustache routine. It was acting. I got it out of an old book I read, *Our Brutal Friend* or *Little Worritt* or something –'

Fergus cut him short: 'And the Raffle money you took? The money for poor animals?'

Silence.

'Well – what's taken you then? Cat got your tongue?'

'All right,' said Vincent. 'It was stupid. I don't see what all the fuss is about though. *Poor* animals, *poor* animals, what about me? Anyhow most of those so-called poor animals are just bone-lazy. Why don't they get out and find a job of work? Makes me sick all that . . .'

'That's enough! More than enough!' Emily's long white tail flicked and whipped. 'Go away! Go away *now*!'

Vincent, looking startled, began creeping off.

'Not yet you don't,' cried Fergus. 'Not after that. There's something we have to do. Ready, boys?'

They were ready. The Tiger Toms began circling

round the big black cat, nodding and nodding, yellow eyes glaring, backs arched, fur on end, claws out, a terrifying sight. Vincent, shaking, covered his face with his paws.

'Leave me alone. She said leave me alone. I haven't done anything.'

But now Fergus gave the dreaded hiss-signal and all the Tiger Toms opened their throats in one high, piercing, screeching hiss, a fearsome noise, an awful moment. Vincent, pale and trembling, almost shrank into the ground.

They stopped, then watched him coldly as he slunk away, a broken cat. Emily shuddered a little, then brightened up and smiled at Fergus; and all the cats in the wood now calmed down and began talking quietly and cheerfully. There was some humming amongst them.

'So it's back to the Ball, is it?' said Fergus. And he and the Bottle Rabbit picked up the heavy Raffle bag.

As they walked back, Francis chattered away to Norman. 'Oh yes. His parents have a big haberdashery back in Bilston. They do very well. I dare say you noticed his black silk socks. Money-mad, Vincent was. Couldn't keep his paws out of the till. Smoked cigarettes behind the bike sheds at school, rude to Mrs Relph, no good at algebra – that sort of thing. Good dancer, mind you, and very good at French . . .'

Near the cricket ground they found the Golden Baker waiting for them under a flowering hazelnut tree. 'Got him, have you?' The Golden Baker wiped his lips.

'Yes, but Emily said let him go. They hissed him

out of the forest, though. He won't forget that in a hurry.' Francis giggled: Fergus said nothing.

The Golden Baker clearly wished he'd seen all this, but he looked happier when he saw the missing Raffle bag.

Then Emily nudged the Bottle Rabbit. She'd caught a glimpse of the departing trickster lurking behind the Tiger Toms' bus, his tail flopping on the ground. The Bottle Rabbit gazed over at him thoughtfully. 'You know, Emily, I feel sort of sorry for him now.'

'For whom?'

'For him, for Raoul.'

'Raymond, you mean, or rather Vincent. Why sorry for him?'

'Well, he looked so bedraggled, empty, absolutely fed up.' The Bottle Rabbit hesitated. 'He looked – he looked like a half-let-down balloon – sort of crumply.'

Emily glanced at the Bottle Rabbit for a moment. 'Well, he certainly deserved that terrible hiss-out. But yes, I see what you mean.'

Now they were back at the Ball. A great cheer went up as an elderly Booge wheeled up his bombardon and the band's bassoons and bagpipes struck into the Good Night Waltz.

Philippe and Josette waltzed slowly and nobly past them, with friendly nods; the bombardon oom-pa-pa'd away.

'Thank goodness he wasn't really French,' whispered Emily.

But the Bottle Rabbit was hunching his shoulders, raising his eyebrows and spreading his paws.

'*On danse?*'* he said, bowing from the waist.
Emily laughed. '*Pourquoi pas?*'† she purred.

With that the Bottle Rabbit put his woolly paw
around Emily's slim waist and she swept and he
stumbled out on to the dance-floor for one last go.

* Shall we dance?
† Why not?

Bottle Rabbit Goes North

'*Bother*,' exclaimed the Bottle Rabbit.

He'd just dropped a perfectly good slice of toast buttered-side-down into Emily's coal-scuttle. A hammering knock on the door of her beech-tree home had startled him; it was the two badger-girls coming in, cheerful but rather noisy animals. 'We're here,' they'd bellowed, and he'd dropped his breakfast toast. Now he picked it up.

'It's just an accident, I'll scrape the slack off,' he said, scraping away.

'Hello Dorothy and hello Margaret; here's a new slice of toast for you, Bottle Rabbit.' Emily bustled in from her kitchen. 'Better forget that coaly one. No use trying to clean *that*.'

The rabbit laughed as he nibbled his new toast (he loved toast). 'She's getting on to me about my Magic Bottle's being dirty again,' he said to the badgers.

'Well,' Emily smiled, 'don't you honestly think it's looking a touch grubby?'

'Looks all right to me. Just a few paw-marks and bits of dust . . .'

'Exactly. And you never know *who* may be looking at it next; all sorts of people.'

'What people? Oh all right, I suppose it could do with a bit of a clean.'

So the kind white cat was soon humming and shaking her head as she washed and polished her friend's Magic Bottle. 'There. I'll put it on the windowsill to dry.' Bright green light shone through the Bottle in the early autumn sun.

Now a great blaring outside made them all race to Emily's front door. The Booge People were arriving for their concert, dozens and dozens and dozens of the hairy little musicians, leaping and dancing and singing as they marched in a surging mass, bassoons and bagpipes leading the way, everybody pushing their instruments on large pram-like wheels. They made a shattering roar of music, like a high wind at sea.

'*Hooray*,' shouted the four animals as they stood there watching and listening.

'Wonderful music,' shouted the Bottle Rabbit. He turned to the badgers. 'You know those Booges pretty well, don't you?'

'Oh, yes, they're great friends of ours, aren't they, Dorothy?'

'Friendship is golden,' said Dorothy.

'And they're awfully nice,' went on Margaret, 'they love chatting and gossiping. And what harm? Of course, *they* call it "kellering" because it's all done by music.'

'By music?' The Bottle Rabbit looked puzzled.

'Yes, the Booges keller back and forth on their instruments all day long, don't they, Dorothy?'

'Lovely long hair he's got,' said Dorothy.

By now the Booges had stopped marching and were just milling about. 'Listen. They're kellering now. It's most interesting,' went on Margaret, 'for instance that big Booge over there with the bassoon, he's talking about the weather, thinks it's going to rain.' They heard the loud bassoon go 'plop, plop, plop'. 'And those bass fiddles, you can hear them grumbling away on the E-string about the bass drums being too heavy.' As they listened one cheerful bass-drum Booge replied with a sprightly 'Pom, tiddley-om-pom. Pom, pom.' 'Of course when they're back at home it's quite different, isn't it, Dorothy?' said Margaret.

'Home, home on the range,' sang Dorothy.

'Oh yes,' said Margaret, 'at home it's all violins, violas, cellos. That's their house-kellering. Strings for everything: string duos, string trios, string quartets, string quintets, string sextets, string septets, string octets, string nonets, string – I forget what comes next, but it's strings for everything private and at home, isn't it, Dorothy?'

'The A Major,' said Dorothy.

'Isn't she a case?' Margaret winked at the others. 'She's soft on one of those cello-Booges. He plays bassoon in the marchings, cello in the privacy of the home.'

'Zoom, zoom, *zoom* – ' began Dorothy, making cello noises, when there came a gasp from the Bottle Rabbit, and a heartfelt *'Bother'*.

Loud though the music and Margaret and Dorothy's voices had been, the rabbit's sharp ears had caught behind him a faint click. He swung round and – his Magic Bottle had disappeared. 'It's gone all right. *Bother.*' The rabbit raced to the window, plunged his head out, stared left, right, centre, up, down – nothing. 'Somebody's got my Bottle. They've got my Bottle – '

Wordlessly cat, rabbit, badger and badger leapt out into the woods and began a search – through the trees, under the bushes, among the dead leaves, in the dustbin, behind the shed, searching and searching. Time passed, nothing turned up; then silently cat and badgers trailed back to sit on Emily's outside wooden bench, and to stare at the Bottle Rabbit, who had flung himself despondently to the ground.

101

'Now what?' he groaned. It was a bad situation. For one thing all the usual stand-by friends were again far away; Fred and Charlie off on a four-day haulage job, Sam the Bear playing in the Mixed Doubles with Maud at the Annual Bears' Picnic Weekend, the Golden Baker baking for a hamsters' wedding, the Golden Eagle at yet another crucial high-speed-bird conference. 'What are we going to do?' the rabbit said miserably. 'We're all on our own.'

Yet help was already at hand. As he lay there with his sad head on the ground an ant came scurrying up to his long left ear. 'Hello, hello, I can help you a little you know,' it squeaked. 'I'm Maurice, I saw a bird, I saw a bird. Most interesting. Black-and-white. Scots accent, Scots accent. I'm Maurice. It flew north, it flew north.'

'What on earth do you mean?' said the Bottle Rabbit, perking up a bit.

'With a green bottle, with a green bottle,' squeaked the ant.

'*Hooray*,' shouted the Bottle Rabbit. 'Which way's north?'

'Up there, up there,' squeaked Maurice, pointing up the lane.

'Come on, Emily, let's go. Thank you, Maurice.'

'Hold on,' said Emily, 'I'll put what food is left in a knapsack.' And the white cat got together what there was, just some jam sandwiches and a bottle of water.

The badger girls had to say goodbye; they were wanted at home for marmalade-making.

'Goodness, I do hope you find that Bottle,' said Margaret.

102

'He really loves his marmalade,' said Dorothy.

And so the anxious cat and rabbit plodded off by themselves on what was to be an odd adventure, full of ups and downs.

They plodded north in silence for miles and miles, until Emily, who'd been thinking hard, suddenly called a halt. 'Wait a minute,' she cried, 'I once met a black-and-white bird with a Scots accent – Hamish MacPie was his name.' On they plodded.

Then, 'Well, there's two black-and-white birds flapping about, just over there,' said the Bottle Rabbit, pointing, 'perhaps one's him. Why don't you ask?'

'You know, I do believe it is – er – excuse me,' Emily spoke loudly, blushing a bit, 'excuse me, aren't you Hamish MacPie?'

'I wouldna say I wasna,' called the bigger black-and-white bird.

'*Hooray*,' shouted the Bottle Rabbit. 'Have you seen my green Bottle?'

'Green Bottle is it? Och aye, I had a wee green bottle in my possession the day.'

'*Hooray*,' shouted the Bottle Rabbit.

'Picked it up the morn's morn. Near a beech tree wha' the wind had blown it.' Hamish cocked an eye at the two of them. 'Glittery wee thing it was. Most interesting. I gave it to a fine wee collie dog in a lorry, in exchange for a bar of chocolate –'
'*Bother*,' interjected the Bottle Rabbit – 'I love the chocolate and ma bonnie lassie, Ailsa, here, she loves the bonnie bright siller wrapping *round* the chocolate. A fine wee Welsh collie he was. Huw, they call him; his gawcie tail wi' upward

103

curl, hung owre his hurdies wi' a swirl.'

'Where did Huw go?' cried both animals.

'I dinna ken *wha* he went. But it was north he was gannin'. He was gannin' north.' Hamish pointed up the road, looking at them pawkily the while.

Both animals braced themselves and started to plod on. 'Dinna fash ye'sels the nu',' called Hamish after them. They didn't say anything back. They couldn't think of anything to say.

Now darkness was looming, so they decided to stop and eat their jam sandwiches and drink their water. 'Oh, how I wish I had my Bottle,' sighed the rabbit wistfully, 'I could pongle up a lovely supper and then we could fly home.'

Emily got really depressed now. 'It's all my fault. I shouldn't have been so bossy, cleaning it up and leaving it on the windowsill like that.'

But the Bottle Rabbit put a comforting black paw round her delicate white waist. 'You only acted for the best, Emily, acted for the best.'

Luckily it was a warm night so they were quite comfortable lying under a lime tree with the stars twinkling through the branches and with peaceful woodland night noises lulling them gently asleep.

Towards morning an owl flew up and landed silently above them in the lime-tree branches, and, 'Halloo, halloo, down there, who are you, who are you? The name's Basil, by the way.'

Sleepily they explained who they were, Emily laying careful stress on the lost Bottle.

Basil's enormous yellow eyes stared unblinking. 'Lost a bottle, have you? Now this raises some most interesting questions. One. How do

you know that this object still exists? Two. Can it still be *there* when you can't actually look at it? Three. Perhaps, then, it's just an *idea* that you have lost?' Cat and rabbit looked at one another sleepily.

'Hoo. Hoo,' hooted the owl, 'I'll have to tease that one out some other time. Now, when did you last see this bugle of yours?' The two animals raised a sleepy protest. '*Not* a bugle? A bottle? Ah *ha*. Well, the principle's the same. "Bottle" is just a name you choose to give the thing, not the thing in itself.' Basil blinked rapidly seven times. 'As it happens I had a "bottle" in my own claws only an hour ago. It fell off the back of a lorry. The lorry was crammed full of bottles, including at least ten green bottles. I remember saying to myself: "If one green bottle should accidently fall –"'

'A green bottle,' shouted the Bottle Rabbit, dancing about, wide-awake now. 'Was it small? Please say it was small.'

'Yes, yes, a small green bottle, though – '

'*Hooray*,' shouted the Bottle Rabbit.

'Where is it?' cried Emily.

'Now, I said it fell accidentally, yet *is* there such a thing as an accident? I doubt it; though you *could* say the bottle was accidentally green – '

'*Where is it?*' both animals yelled.

'I gave it to Bert, the schoolmaster.'

'*Bother*,' said the Bottle Rabbit.

'He seemed to think it would be useful for observation in the classroom tomorrow. I pointed out that it all depends on what you mean by obser–'

'Who's Bert? Where's Bert?'

'Don't fuss me. Well, he's a bulldog, like most schoolmasters, and he lives in the schoolhouse up on the moor.'

'*Hooray*,' shouted the Bottle Rabbit. 'Where's that?'

'A long way up north, a long way up north.'

'*Bother*,' said the Bottle Rabbit.

Basil the Owl now snapped shut his huge yellow eyes and went straight to sleep.

They collected their things and plodded off north. To their right the sun was rising, and all around them birds were chanting their morning choruses, flowers were opening their petals to the grateful new light. Emily and the Bottle Rabbit, however, were tired and hungry and footsore and sad.

Their long journey now took them far up into the beautiful bare moorlands clothed only in purple heather, in green bracken. They had no eyes for it all, but their four ears did catch the clanking of a cracked bell; it came from a distant square-built stone schoolhouse where small animals with satchels were crowding in.

The two searchers crept up quietly. Through a window they could clearly see a bulldog, surely Bert. He was talking to his class. He was holding something up. He was pointing to it. It was the Magic Bottle.

'*Hooray*,' whispered the Bottle Rabbit, and made a little bound towards the window, but Emily held him back with a gentle white paw.

'Wait and see, Bottle Rabbit, wait and see. At all costs we must not disturb his class.'

'*Bother*,' whispered the Bottle Rabbit.

Bert was talking loudly: 'This small bottle, boys and girls, can teach us much about the world we live in, much about the world we live in. Put away that catapult, Craig, and do pay attention. You too, Wendy, and stop *whispering*, Andrew. Note its colour, everybody. Grace, what colour is this bottle? Green? Yes, quite right, green. Very good, Grace. And what is this bottle for? *Gin*? Tom, I'm surprised at you. And anyhow one's usual gin bottle is quite a bit fatter and – Ahem. Well. You all give up? Nobody knows? Ah *ha*. Then that will be a little task for you. Find out by tomorrow. Also for tomorrow I propose a little essay – ' groans from the class – '"Adventures of a Bottle", most interesting. Remember now, no blots, everything neat – '

A bell clanged. 'All right. Good. Off with you to the gymnasium. Quietly.' He sent them out in batches. 'First six animals – Christopher, put the bottle down – Next six animals – Paul, wake up –

Next six animals – That's enough, Hugo –' They crowded out. 'Quietly now the rest of you.' Crash. Bash. And the room was empty. The bull-dog sighed and went out too.

The Bottle Rabbit said, *'Hooray,'* under his breath and started to climb in through the class-room window. Then, *'Bother,'* as he dropped back. The door had opened yet again, this time to let in a crusty-looking old sheepdog with a broom. This dog swept the dust about a bit, then stopped and stared at the Bottle.

'I'll tak' that for me pills. Me back-pills.' And he slipped it in his pocket. Cat and rabbit stared at one another aghast. The grumpy sheepdog peered at a fusee clock on the wall. 'Eleven o'clock. Time for me scrag. Time for me scrag.' He put down his broom, left the schoolhouse, mounted a high old black bicycle and pedalled off northwards through the lovely countryside.

'*Now* what?'

'Well, we'll have to follow him.'

108

The sheepdog looked so fierce and surly, they didn't dare say anything, just lolloped along behind as he bicycled on. At last he reached a little bridge arching over a moorland beck (or stream), dismounted, took out some bread and cheese from a newspaper, sat on a rock and began to munch. As he munched he took up the Bottle and began talking to himself.

'You'd be surprised what it says on the bottoms of bottles,' he said, 'different things, dates and that; it's a study.' The sheepdog slowly settled half-spectacles on the end of his surly nose. 'Let's see. Yes. It says summat here. Most interesting, I expect. "This truth only bear in mind. I'm only useful to the Kind."' The dog wrinkled his big nose. 'What's that supposed to mean then? Kind? What kind? Kind of what? Stumps me. But it's a study.'

Standing nearby, watching all this, and listening to all this, the Bottle Rabbit began nudging Emily. But now a sudden frightening dark mist fell over everything. It was so thick and dark that cat and rabbit could scarcely see the ends of their little noses, let alone the sheepdog. The moor became eerie and silent, and in a panic they clutched one another, hearts beating fast. They were alone in the dark in a strange, strange place. And there came an odd scuffling, thumping noise. Dim figures loomed, and loud voices sounded, very close to them:

'It's a reet thick 'un, Maisie.'

'Reet enough, Jack.'

There was hoarse breathing, and the two young animals gasped. Who could it be? Or what could it be?

109

Now at last a pleasant surprise. A gust of wind, the mist swirling away from them, and there stood two handsome Airedales, crisp and firm in their black-and-brown curled woolly coats. It was Jack and Maisie, of all people, old friends of theirs; Maisie a warm, motherly figure, Jack a younger, wilder but also very good-hearted animal, Maisie's nephew, in fact.

'Maisie, Jack, help us,' they cried.

'Of course, of course,' barked the reliable Airedales.

Cat and rabbit quickly explained the position.

'*What* bad-tempered sheepdog's got his paws on your Bottle?' growled Maisie.

They turned to point the sheepdog out when, '*Bother*,' said the Bottle Rabbit, 'can't see a thing.' Again there was fog all around them, as if they were up in a balloon, and hanging in the misty clouds.

'This really is peculiar,' said Emily.

'Oh aye, it's what we call a North Roak, down our end,' barked Jack. 'There's nowt as clethery as a North Roak when it comes up off t'moor, like. Maisie'll tell, thee, won't tha, lass?'

Maisie nodded. 'Aye, all a body can do is get whoam, put t'wood in t'hole and glamber down for t'night, when t'North Roak's heavy on t'moor.'

The Bottle Rabbit nodded and smiled as hard as he could, though not quite sure what his two North Country friends were actually saying.

'It's the mist,' whispered Emily.

'That's reet, lass, reet first time,' barked Jack. 'Tha s'll not find much o' that down south, I'll reckon.'

110

Now with another light swirl of wind the mist cleared and the sun shone once again, revealing the scowling old sheepdog, standing by the rushing beck. Jack stared over at him. 'Well, I'll be jaggered if it bain't owd Blake from down High Baxton,' he barked. 'He'll give t'bottle back and glad to.'

'*Hooray*,' shouted the Bottle Rabbit.

Jack raced over to Blake, and a loud slow barking began, back and forth. Sheepdog and Airedale were both sounding fierce, but Emily could see some steady tail-wagging going on. The slow back-and-forth went something like this:

'BAHT BAUKY BAT, LAD.'
'MAHT CLABBER.'
'CLAR DAG BAGGER ON ME TOD?'
'BLAD BLAGGERT BAHT MUG.'
'CLABBERT LAG LAIKIN ABAOUT?'
'NOWT BLAD THISEN. FUSTILUGS.'

Here Jack guffawed but Blake's stiff face never changed. They went on barking at each other like this for some time. Then the sheepdog without change of countenance handed back the Bottle, nodded to Maisie, Emily and the Bottle Rabbit, slowly got back on to his high black bike and rode slowly back to the schoolhouse.

'RAHT BAG CLABBERT BLADGE NORTH ROAK,' barked Jack after him. Blake turned round on his bicycle saddle and:

'NOWT OUT CLABBERT BLAG EMSLI,' came clattering back across the moor.

Now Jack raced towards them with the Magic

Bottle. 'He's a gradely lad, our Blake,' he was barking, and then, "Here's thi bottle, lad.'

'*Hooray*,' the Bottle Rabbit began to shout. But Jack in his hurry had stumbled over a boulder and the Magic Bottle went flying into the air. '*Bother*,' shouted the Bottle Rabbit in despair. Would it smash itself into smithereens on the beckside stones after all this? Would they have to plod home without it?

This might well have been, but for Airedale resourcefulness. As the animals all gasped, Maisie leapt forward and caught the shining treasure in her outstretched paws.

'*Hooray*,' shouted the Bottle Rabbit, and Emily sighed with relief. 'At last, at last,' she murmured.

'Well, then,' panted Jack, as the rabbit stroked the Bottle fervently with his black woolly paws, 'tha's got thi Bottle now, reet enough. Art thinkin' o' stayin' up north, like, now tha's got here?'

'As a matter of fact, Jack, we're pretty hungry,' said the Bottle Rabbit.

'Nowt wrong wi' that. Our Maisie'll bek up a batch o' barmcakes and some baps and that, and ah'll mek a pot o' tea.'

'That's very kind of both of you,' said Emily, 'but I think the Bottle Rabbit has something special in mind.'

She was right: 'Pongle ... Pongle ... Pongle ... Pongle ... Pongle ... Pongle ... Pongle ... Pongle.' The rabbit was pongling away like mad, and getting excellent results, for soon all four animals were sitting by the beck and tucking into a substantial picnic: roast chicken, boiled ham, cheese, pork pies, pickles and, because they were up north, baps, dropped scones, pikelets and barmcakes. The two Airedales were surprised and almost certainly pleased; though, being from the North, all they said was: 'Not bad food' (Maisie), and 'Pass us a pie, then, lass' (Jack).

But at last the Bottle was safe and the rabbit could lie contentedly in the warm, springy heather, munching a bap, listening to the beck babbling away across the moor, sniffing the rich peat smoke from some distant farmhouse chimney.

'Oh Emily, so much has happened since I dropped that toast,' he said, 'and do you realize we've missed the Booge People's Concert? But never mind, they'll do other concerts, and it's so lovely up north.'

'Let's stay up north for a few days then,' said Emily; 'that is, if our Airedale friends won't mind?'

'We'll put up with you,' said Jack.

So they did stay, and went exploring all over the moors for three whole days, with lots of pongled-up picnics and evening singsongs around Maisie's fireplace. It was their biggest outing, ever.

When it came time to go home, the Bottle Rabbit proposed the Twelve Mice and their carriage, so that they could travel back in style along the same road that they'd plodded so unhappily up. Emily agreed and – 'Pongle . . . Pongle . . . Pongle . . . Pongle . . . Pongle,' went the rabbit. (He could hardly stop himself from pongling now, in his happiness.)

Even the Airedales for once looked astonished

113

when up whirled that elegant little state carriage with its spangling wheels and charming interior, drawn by ten powerful and cheerful mice, with one outrider and the postilion, Nigel, at the reins. 'Well, all I'll say is we never see nowt like this up our end,' said Jack, as the two Airedales waved goodbye.

'Are we *still* going north?' asked the Bottle Rabbit. In fact they were now trundling speedily back home.

'Well, not really,' said Emily, 'but what a lot of different places we've seen in the last few days.'

'And what a lot of different people there have been,' said the rabbit: 'badger, Booge, ant, Scots bird, Welsh collie, owl, bulldog, sheepdog, Airedale – ' his voice trailed off.

'*And* mouse, AND pigeon, lovey,' cooed someone.

They gasped. Norman's shapely head had appeared, upside-down, at the coach window. 'Hello, my dears. Yes – it's little me. I'm taking the

liberty of travelling up top with my friend Nigel.
Keeping the driver company, aren't I, Nige?' They
heard the big, smartly-uniformed mouse give a
loud tootle on his coachman's bugle in reply. 'Isn't
he a *tease*? I do believe Nige thinks *he*'s a Booge,
half the time. Well, goodbye for now, darlings;
see you-all back at the ranch.' Norman popped
out of sight, then reappeared. 'Nige says that,
barring accidents, we'll be back home by bedtime.' He gave them a huge wink and fluttered
away again. '*Hooray*,' mumbled both animals
drowsily as they sank back on the plush red
cushions.

Soon they were safely home. And, it turned
out, so were all the Bottle Rabbit's other friends.
Every one of them, including Maurice, was most
interested in what had been going on. As they sat
round the fire at Fred and Charlie's, drinking
mostly cocoa, there was much to tell about their
strange journey north, and their various accidents. All was quiet now, though they knew there
were still some Booges about in the woods,
because the summer night breeze brought with it
a faint honk of bombardons, a gentle rattle of
musical bones. The Bottle Rabbit was really tired;
he yawned as he told them about Booge-kellering,
and how he and Emily had had to scuttle north
again and again in search of his Bottle, and he got
so drowsy as he toasted his toes by the coal fire,
that he didn't even bother to get to the end of it all
before falling fast asleep.

7

Bottle Rabbit Hits Town

One October day the Bottle Rabbit's taut woolly body came half tumbling down the stairs of a dark gold double-decker bus. Luckily the conductor, a good-natured young water spaniel, caught him neatly at the bottom, or the confused rabbit might well have gone head-over-heels into the gutter in Corporation Road.

'Hold hard, young feller-me-lad,' said the spaniel cheerfully, as he held on to the rabbit with one paw and straightened his own peaked cap with the other. 'No need to hurry. We're not there yet.'

'Is this – isn't this the Town Hall?' gasped the Bottle Rabbit, who had only ever been into the town once before, to see the pantomime when he was quite small.

'That's right. This was, is, and we hope always will be our noble Town Hall,' cried the spaniel in ringing tones. 'And it's full of noble servants of the people, all drinking tea, I shouldn't wonder, at our expense.' Various animals inside the bus laughed approvingly, and the spaniel looked pleased.

'May I get off, then?' said the Bottle Rabbit meekly.

'Soon as we've stopped, you can. But not

before. I think we've had enough acrobatics for one Monday morning.' All the animals laughed again, and the Bottle Rabbit felt shy. He was not used to these quick city ways and also he didn't understand about the tea.

He was on his way to meet his old Clydesdale friend, Fred, who had some business to attend to first. They were going to eat in a café, something he'd hardly ever done, and go to the cinema, and then spend the night at Fred's Aunt Norah's house. Charlie had given the Bottle Rabbit detailed instructions and put him on the early bus, thinking it might be nice for him to potter about the town, see the park, the museum, perhaps even the famous Transporter Bridge, before meeting Fred at four o'clock.

The huge grey Town Hall was easily a hundred years old, with Gothic spires and mullioned windows. The rabbit stared up at it, impressed, but also confused as he felt himself being pushed and shoved by a hurrying throng of busy animals; dogs, cats, beavers, badgers, pigeons, ducks, horses, cows, geese, otters, guinea fowl in enormous numbers were pressing along, some silent and moody, most talking fast and loud, looking at watches, catching buses, crossing the road, getting and spending and shouting and running. It all seemed so far away from forest life – Fred and Charlie in their cabin, Emily in her tree, the Golden Baker slowly pedalling through the quiet woods with his three-wheeled cartload of buns. When a gang of noisy turkeys from the railway station came gobbling along the street towards him the Bottle Rabbit hopped on to the spacious

117

Town Hall steps. Here a handsome bulldog, who turned out to be the Mayor, was addressing a group of dachshunds, all dressed in square dark suits. He was telling them about the town's bus and railway stations. Two hares in smart business suits strode by with their briefcases.

'Sailors off a ship,' said one of them, pointing to the dachshunds. 'Just come in from abroad.'

'Got up in their best for the visit, I suppose,' said the other. 'Foreigners.'

The dachshunds were all listening politely and nodding a lot as the Mayor spoke, or rather barked, at length. Then, 'Any questions about what I've said so far?' The dachshunds went on nodding and looking polite, but asked nothing. The truth is they hadn't understood a word the Mayor had said, being foreign.

'All right, then, now I'll tell you about our well-

118

known Dorman Museum and Albert Park.' And he told them all about that. Then he told them all about the public library. Then he told them about the List of Mayors on a plaque on a wall in the Town Hall. And he told them the names of some of the mayors. Then he asked if they'd like to see his mayor's gold chain. When no one spoke he showed it to them anyhow. It was hanging round his neck – a big heavy gold chain. 'It's got all the mayors' names on it, carved,' he barked. 'It's got *my* name on it.' He turned to his assistant Mayor, also a bulldog.

'Should I tell 'em about the mayor's official car, Bob? They don't seem to say anything.'

'Shouldn't if I was you,' said Bob. 'I'd stop if I was you, Ray. Besides, it's twelve o'clock, nearly. It's time for dinner.'

'So it is,' grunted the Mayor, his voice hoarse from speech-making. 'I lose count of time, you know, it's all so interesting. Come on, all of you.' And he led the way up the steps and into the Town Hall. All the dachshunds crowded in after the Mayor. Bob, the assistant Mayor, saw the Bottle Rabbit standing there, looking lost, his black woolly body tense.

'Come on; you too,' he said in a gruff but friendly voice. 'Plenty for everybody.'

Polite as ever, the Bottle Rabbit decided he had better go in, even though he wasn't a dachshund. He was hungry, as it happened, having got up so early for the bus. Also perhaps it was always like this at Town Halls. Inside he found a big lunch set up in the banquet-room: hot soup (it was a chilly day, the Mayor explained), fresh fried fish (they

119

were not far from the sea, the Mayor explained), and chipped potatoes and cauliflower (there were numerous market gardens in the suburbs, the Mayor explained). The dachshunds made a lot of noise with their soup, as foreign animals will. They liked the fish and chips, but did not seem so keen on the pots of tea that came with the food. They spoke rapidly to each other about it in a foreign tongue. The Bottle Rabbit quietly ate his food and drank his tea.

When the two bulldogs invited the visitors upstairs to see the List of Mayors the Bottle Rabbit slipped out, and following Charlie's early-morning directions, turned right, then left, passed the Élite Cinema and the Gaumont Palace, and after a long walk found the park, which was full of geraniums. Next to it was the museum, a squat building with a green-rusted copper dome.

Near an iron railing outside it he met two oldish sheep who were standing about – rams actually – one short, fat, bespectacled and smiling, the other tall, rangy and melancholy, with watery eyes. Both carried briefcases (the thin one had two), and both had something sharp and city-like about their faces. But they seemed friendly enough.

'Visiting our museum, are you? Good for you, young fellow; we'll come along too,' said the fat ram. And they did. And they were most helpful.

'Mind your head going in,' smiled the fat one. Then he pointed out a picture of the Duke of Wellington with a telescope on a big white horse, and another one of Napoleon, and some French guns and some Prussian guns and some battle scenes from ancient times, and explained all about

them. The thin ram pointed out hundreds of but-
terflies that had been caught and stuck on cards,
and showed him important old pieces of stone
and many seashells. And the fat ram showed him
a beehive where you could see the bees making
honey through a glass window. 'The thin bees
make it and the fat bees eat it,' said the thin ram.
'That's the capitalist system.' The fat ram told him
the seashells were worth millions and millions of
pounds. The thin ram told him one of the bigger
stones had fallen to earth from the planet Jupiter
Pluvius. A lot of what they said sounded strange
and difficult to the Bottle Rabbit, so he had a good
deal of nodding to do. But he enjoyed this
museum visit very much and felt he had never
met such a well-informed pair of animals.

'Mind your boots going out,' said the thin ram.
It was a quarter-to-three and time to go back to the

121

Town Hall, to meet Fred. 'We'll come with you, won't we, Max?' said the fat ram. 'Yes, Arthur, we will,' said the thin one. The two sheep were exchanging many nods and winks over the Bottle Rabbit's long, floppy ears. But he didn't take any notice, because he was thinking how much easier it was to move through the crowds between these two experienced city-dwellers.

When they got back to the Town Hall Max looked up at it with his watery eyes and sighed. 'I used to be Mayor once,' he said. 'I used to wear the gold chain. My name's on it, same as Ray's.'

'Really?' said the Bottle Rabbit.

Max nodded gloomily. Arthur smiled: 'Oh yes, Max is a very much respected figure in the town. Yes, that very heavy old eighteen-carat gold chain – if only I could get my hands –' He seemed to stop himself. Then, 'Oh, by the way, just to satisfy my curiosity, what's that you have there?' He pointed to the Bottle Rabbit's Bottle-pocket.

The Bottle Rabbit thought, 'Well, why not? They seem friendly, and know so many interesting things.' So he pulled out his precious Magic Bottle. To his surprise Max immediately groaned loudly. 'Oh, *no*,' he moaned. 'It can't be one of *those*? It's not possible. Arthur, we must leave. We're not safe here.' He pointed a trembling hoof at the Bottle.

'What's the problem, Max?' said Arthur. For a moment the Bottle Rabbit thought that Arthur was grinning a little. But Max certainly wasn't grinning. 'Everything's the problem,' he said urgently. 'Let's get out of here! Quick! It's a dangerous situation! I have my health to consider!

I must protect myself! I – I owe it to my constituents! We're not safe, I tell you!'

'What's wrong?' said the Bottle Rabbit, puzzled.

'That Bottle of yours. Just how long have you been in this town, Rabbit?' Max asked sternly.

'I – I got here about half-past-eleven this morning. I came in the bus. But I haven't done anything bad. What's wrong?'

'Mottle-scab's what's wrong – mottle-scab.'

'Oh, *no*!' cried Arthur in his turn.

Max was looking feverishly at his watch. 'And it's nearly half-past-three now. My gracious, that's practically four hours. Four hours' exposure of that Bottle to the town's atmosphere. Don't forget we're an iron and steel town, Rabbit. I know. I used to be Mayor once. It's the blast-furnace fumes. There's a reaction. Any minute now that Bottle will be pouring out mottle-scab on to every passer-by, young and old alike. Come on, Arthur!' He made a visible effort to calm himself. 'You stay where you are for now, Rabbit. And for goodness' sake put that Bottle *away*.' And the two concerned-looking rams seemed poised to leave in a hurry.

'Wait. Oh wait. Please wait,' cried the Bottle Rabbit. 'What'll I do? What *can* I do? Won't you help me?' He looked at them with frightened, pleading eyes.

'Sorry, young rabbit,' said Arthur, still smiling, 'it's every animal for himself now. I know it sounds hard, but – have you ever seen mottle-scab? Horrible. Covers your whole body. And the pain's something awful.' Arthur and Max shuddered.

123

'But you can't just leave me,' cried the Bottle Rabbit piteously.

Max shrugged his narrow shoulders, and the two rams seemed on the point of leaping away when Arthur laid a hoof on Max's shoulder.

'No, Max. No. This rabbit's right, you know. We can't just go off and leave him. It would be un-animal. There must be something we can do.'

Max stopped and scowled and shook his thin head. Then he looked up and growled grudgingly, 'Well, I could try the Wapentake Test.'

'Good idea,' said Arthur.

'What's that?' said the Bottle Rabbit eagerly.

'No time to explain now. It's a risk, of course, but I'll give it a try. Look, put your Bottle in this briefcase. I'll take it and do the Test, and you wait here with Arthur. If I'm not back in fifteen minutes it means I've got the mottle-scab myself and I'm done for.' Max gave a long sigh. 'Here, Arthur, look after my gold watch for me. And you can take my big money-bag, Rabbit.' He handed him his other heavy briefcase. 'If anything happens to me, all that money is yours. It'll be no use to me any more.'

'Oh Max, Max, be careful,' Arthur cried loudly and emotionally.

'I'll do what I have to do; no more and no less,' said Max sternly.

'Thank you. Thank you very much, Max,' said the Bottle Rabbit quietly as the ram plunged off. He stood there holding Max's heavy money-bag for him and when the thin ram had disappeared he and Arthur stared at one another.

'You know, I'd never even heard of mottle-scab before.'

Arthur shuddered. 'Let's not talk about it,' he whispered. 'Poor Max. But he's a terribly clever sheep. He's been Mayor, you know. I really wish I had that big thick gold chain in my hands, this minute.' Arthur's thoughts seemed to have drifted away, but he brought himself back to the Bottle Rabbit. 'Don't worry yourself, young Rabbit. Max'll work something out.'

The Bottle Rabbit half thought he'd like to look at all the money in Max's bag, but then he thought it wouldn't be polite. Instead he asked, 'What exactly *is* the Wapentake Test?'

'What's the what? Oh, that. Well, it's – er – well it's hard to explain. I tell you what. Let's go over there and have an ice-cream while we're waiting.' And Arthur led the Bottle Rabbit over to Scappaticci's red, white and green ice-cream cart, where they each had a large vanilla cornet. Then they waited. After a while the Town Hall clock boomed the three-quarters. It was now quarter-to-four and still no sign of Max. 'At least good old Fred'll be here soon,' thought the Bottle Rabbit to himself wearily.

A loud commotion down the street, and – 'Here's Max! It's Max! Good for you, Max!' Arthur called, leaping about plumply. 'He does it every time; how did it go, Max?' The thin dark ram came bounding unsmilingly back, panting a little.

'Caught it just in time. The Test did the trick. Worked perfect. Look.' He handed the Bottle back to the Bottle Rabbit, who gave Max his briefcase and with a smile of relief started to look carefully at his Bottle. It looked much the same as ever to him, greenish, smallish, perhaps a bit less dusty.

125

'Well, I'm really glad it worked. That Test, I mean. What did you call it again?' But the thin ram was muttering something to Arthur, who was grinning delightedly. Max then swung round, staring rather fiercely. 'The Test? Oh, yes, the Test. Of course I used the Wapplebreaker Test.'

'Oh? It sounded different before,' said the Bottle Rabbit, 'but the main thing is it worked and there's no more danger of . . .'

'Of mottle-blain? No, that's all been taken care of.'

'But what about the mottle-*scab*?'

'That too,' interrupted Arthur hurriedly. 'Look, we have to be off now. Glad we could help.'

'But shouldn't I pay you something for the Test . . .' began the Bottle Rabbit.

'Pay?' said Max, stopping, though Arthur was trying to pull him away. 'Well, how much have you got?'

The Bottle Rabbit looked in his little brown purse. 'I've got ninety p. But I'll need fifty for the bus home.'

'Hold it, Arthur! Stop pulling me about. Hold it! Ninety p., eh? Yes. Well, you'd better give me that,' said Max, taking it all and pocketing it.

'Come *on*,' said Arthur impatiently, and he bounded away, with Max now leaping after him. At that very moment a familiar clop-clop-clop revealed that Fred must be near. 'Funny those two didn't say goodbye,' said the Bottle Rabbit to himself. 'Still, they did help me. I wish Fred could have met them. He'd have liked them a lot.'

Fred now came galloping up and soon he and the Bottle Rabbit were having sausages and chips and sharing a pot of strong tea in the café opposite the Town Hall. Of course the Bottle Rabbit immediately told Fred all about his new sheep friends and the mottle-scab danger and the success of the Test. 'Narrow escape, wasn't it, Fred?' ended the Bottle Rabbit. Fred, who had seemed a bit fidgety during all this, asked the waitress for extra vinegar and said nothing for a while. Then, 'Bottle Rabbit, mind if I take a look at your Bottle?'

'Of course not.' He pulled it out. Fred filled and carefully lit his curly old pipe and, puffing slowly, held the Bottle up to the light and stared at it. Then he shook his big head slightly.

'Bottle Rabbit,' he said, 'I want you to do something for me. Try a pongle. Pongle up some lemonade. Or rather, no; they mightn't like it in here. Bad for business, perhaps. Let's go outside.'

Fred paid the bill and the Bottle Rabbit followed him outside; a dull apprehension was beginning to stir in his woolly breast. He pulled out the cork, looked at Fred, bent over the Bottle and pongled once: 'Pongle.' The two animals waited. Nothing. 'Try sandwiches, then,' said Fred. The Bottle Rabbit pongled twice. Again they waited. Again – nothing. 'Try the Blue Hares. Try the mice. Try the Golden Eagle General Alarum. – Oh, Bottle Rabbit, what's the use?' cried Fred. They looked at one another. The Bottle Rabbit's eyes grew bigger and bigger. He swallowed a lump in his throat.

'Those two old sheep tricked me,' he said at last, very quietly and miserably. 'They took my real Bottle and left this – this stupid old useless old ordinary green bottle instead. It was all a trick.'

'Yes, a confidence trick, I'm afraid. And a very

neat one,' said Fred. 'And they took all your money, too.' He slowly lit another pipe, puffed at it and then said decisively, 'First, they're bound to bungle the pongle. Second, we are going to meet fire with fire. Let's see, didn't you say one of them used to be Mayor once?'

'Yes, Max was,' said the Bottle Rabbit sadly.

'All right. First stop the Town Hall,' said Fred. And they hurried up those broad steps and into an office marked 'Inquiries'. Fred was soon talking away earnestly to a concerned young squirrel in a black alpaca jacket, with pens behind both ears.

'You desire a list of mayors' addresses? Old mayors' addresses?' said the little squirrel. 'Yet there are so many old mayors. It would be much easier if you could furnish me with a description, or a name, you know.'

'Well, in the first place he was a sheep, and in the second place he was called . . .'

'A sheep? I do not recall any sheep-mayors. It has been mostly bulldogs and weasels . . . Oh, bless my soul! Wait a minute. He was not a long, thin, stringy, grumpy-looking gawdelpus of an animal, was he?'

'Sounds like Max,' said Fred.

'Max? Did you say Max?' The little squirrel laughed heartily. 'Him Mayor? Not likely. We've had some funny ones all right, in our time, but we're not *that* badly off. Max did have a temporary job here once. They made him second-assistant typewriter-repairer, I think it was. But not for long. He messed up the keys. Twisted the ribbons. They had to get rid of him. He's always hanging around at the bus-station and at the museum with his fat friend Arthur.'

'They're the ones,' said the two animals in one voice.

'Want to see them, do you? Well, it's up to you. Not much to my taste, either of 'em. But what you do is catch the C bus. Go past the village and get off at the end of the Crescent at Oxford Road. Turn right – that's Roman Road – go past the shops – there's a red post office and a white dairy – and turn left into Rockliffe Road and they're halfway down. It's a green house. I forget what number, but it's the only house with a poplar tree in front of it. Take you about twenty minutes. One thing, though. Don't tell 'em I sent you, whatever you do.'

129

They thanked the little squirrel and went and stood outside. Up rumbled a blue double-decker. 'It's a C. This is our bus, Bottley,' said Fred. They sat in front at the top. Unhappy though he was, the Bottle Rabbit liked very much having Fred with him in the town. Fred knew what to say and do all the time. He was confident and strong and sensible.

Before long they were standing in Rockliffe Road outside a terrace house with a tall poplar tree in front. Fred moved quietly up to the bow window, stared past a big aspidistra for a moment and then clopped quietly back. 'They're in there all right,' he said, 'just as I thought, pongling. Pongling like mad. Didn't notice a thing.'

The Bottle Rabbit heaved a great weary sigh. It all seemed so dismal and unnecessary: bad animals taking his Bottle and then not being able to make it work, because of Unkindness. 'Look,' said Fred, 'I know how you feel. Take this twenty p., and go and have a glass of milk and a bun at that dairy in Roman Road. I think I know what to do here. I'll meet you at the dairy in ten minutes.'

The Bottle Rabbit nodded gratefully and scampered off as Fred turned back to the house. The great cart-horse quickly gave a thunderous knock on the door with his powerful front hooves. It opened slowly. The short, fat ram was standing there, his glasses gleaming, rather out of breath, looking bad-tempered, but still trying to smile his big smile.

'Yes? What is it?' said Arthur, looking up at Fred.

'I'm from the Housing,' said Fred in a firm voice. 'We need to measure your front room. It's for the Rent Assurance Register. It won't take me a minute.' As he spoke he pushed past Arthur and moved quickly into the front room, where Max was scowling at a card-table on which, in the middle of a Benares tray, stood the little green Magic Bottle.

'Here. What do *you* want? Who are you? What are you doing here?' snarled Max.

'Housing-Assurance-Register. Just a check-up. For our files,' said Fred. Then he looked out of the window. 'Well, well. What's that thick leather wallet doing lying under your poplar tree? Looks valuable. Somebody must have ...' But both sheep had already rushed to the window and were peering round the aspidistra. It was child's play for Fred to switch bottles while their fleecy backs were turned.

'What do you mean, wallet? There's no thick wallet out there,' said Arthur pettishly, turning back into the room.

'Oh? Isn't there?' said Fred calmly. 'I must have been mistaken, then. I could have sworn I saw one just now. Well, never mind.' Fred was pacing the room as he spoke. 'Yes. Ye-es. That seems right. Sixteen-by-twelve, as I thought. We'll make a little note of that.' And he took out a notebook and pen and wrote some figures down. 'Well, gentlemen, I think that's all I'll be needing from you. I'll bid you good-day.' Fred moved towards the door and stopped. He looked round the room. 'Nice pictures you have here. Isn't that *The Boyhood of Raleigh* over there?' He pointed to a reproduction of an oil painting on the wall behind the card-table. Then he started, looked down, and stared in astonishment. 'Wait a minute. *Wait* a minute. No, I can't believe it. Are my eyes deceiving me or haven't you fortunate fellows got hold of one of those rare Magic Bottles? I declare I haven't seen one of those in years. Congratulations to you both!'

'It's a bottle – Just a bottle – Old bottle – It's ours – Old green bottle – None of your business – Sauce bottle – Chap gave it me.' Both animals gabbled away desperately and tried to shoo Fred out. But Fred stood firmly there on his great carthorse legs.

'Fascinating. Truly fascinating,' he said at last, 'but where's your tholing-pin?'

'What do you mean, tholing-pin?' snapped Max.

'Well, if it's like the other Magic Bottles *I* know it won't work without a tholing-pin. You've got to hold your tholing-pin in your teeth and roll about on your back with your paws in the air before you start pongling with your Magic Bottle. Surely you know that?'

'We aren't pongling, are we, Max? It's just a bottle,' said Arthur feebly.

'Still, I wouldn't mind having a tholing-pin. Just for interest,' said Max through his gritted teeth, trying to smile at Fred while looking fiercely at Arthur. 'Where do you get them – sir?'

'Well, curiously enough I have one in my possession. It's here in my pocket now,' said Fred. 'Funny. You won't believe this, either of you. I once heard of an animal in the woods who

132

couldn't get his Magic Bottle to work just because
he didn't even know about the tholing-pin. Extraordinary. There he was with a gold-mine in his
hand and he couldn't use it properly. Funny,
really.' Fred laughed.

Neither sheep laughed. Max cleared his throat
and scowled warningly at Arthur. 'I don't suppose you'd care to lend us your tholing-pin, sir? –
Sell it, I mean,' he said hastily, as Fred began to
shake his head.

The Clydesdale seemed to make a quick calcula-
tion. 'Well, I tell you what. They come expensive,
tholing-pins, but I'll make you a real bargain offer,
just because I like your faces so much. How about
three pounds sixty?'

'Ye-es, ye-es, ye-es, ye-es,' baa-ed both sheep in
unison. Arthur produced this sum with shaking
hooves. Fred reached into his nosebag, pulled out
a long black iron nail he'd been carrying about for
some time, and held it out. Max grabbed at it.
'That's a tholing-pin?' he growled.

'Quite right. And a very good specimen. Note
the serrated shaft.'

'You hold it in your teeth?' said Arthur.

'Quite right,' said Fred. 'And don't forget to roll
about a good deal. Give it, say, ten, fifteen
minutes rolling about, the first couple of times.
Then you can cut down. Well, I have to be going.
I've still got Roman Road to do.'

And Fred moved quietly out and quietly shut
the door. Behind him he could hear; 'Me first.'
'No, me.' 'It's me got the Bottle.' 'Well I helped.'
'It's not fair.' 'Who says?' 'Daft oyt,' and so on.

Fred soon found the Bottle Rabbit at the dairy,

crumbling a bun in nervous paws. There was milk round his mouth. 'Fred. Fred. What happened?'

Fred winked slowly, patted his pocket, and said, 'All's well. All's very well indeed.'

'Really? *Really*? Oh Fred. Thank you so much,' and the Bottle Rabbit leapt up and down and clapped his paws together. They went off happily to catch the D bus back into town. As they were settling down at the top in front again, Fred said, 'Oh, by the way, this is for you,' and he handed over the Bottle. 'And so is this.' Fred then gave the Bottle Rabbit two pounds ninety p. 'I've kept fifty p. for these bus fares and twenty p. for your milk and bun. Ninety p. is what Max took from you, and the other two pounds can pay for our cinema. I think those unpleasant old rams owe us that much at least.' Then Fred told the delighted Bottle Rabbit how he'd tricked them. 'Confidence trick for confidence trick. Seems reasonable, doesn't it?' And Fred winked his big kindly horse-eye again. 'First I got a free lunch with the Mayor,' said the Bottle Rabbit, laughing, 'then a free film. I'm beginning to like this town-life.'

So they saw an amusing old picture, *Harvey*, with James Stewart, at the Gaumont, and caught one more bus, the M, out to Fred's Aunt Norah, who lived in Orchard Road. As they got near their destination Fred suddenly chuckled. 'That film was funny, I suppose. But I can't help thinking about that fat sheep and that thin sheep, clutching their tholing-pin in their teeth and rolling about on the floor with their paws in the air. Comical. Let's hope they don't catch mottle-scab, or mottle-blain.'

The Bottle Rabbit sat quietly beaming. He was simply overwhelmed with admiration for this splendid cart-horse's wit and wisdom.

'Somebody's looking very pleased with themselves tonight,' remarked the bus-conductor, a hairy Irish terrier, as they got off. The Bottle Rabbit did this rather carefully, remembering his morning difficulties. The terrier smiled pleasantly at them both. 'What happened? Did yez lose a penny and find a pound? Is that it?'

'Something on those lines,' said Fred.

'Well, a very good night to yez both, anyway,' said the Irish terrier as the bus pulled off. 'Good luck now.' Fred and the Bottle Rabbit stood in the gutter and waved goodbye. Various passengers nodded and smiled, including some of that morning's dachshunds, who were sitting there in rows.

'There are plenty of decent animals in this town, too, you know,' remarked Fred, as they crossed the road and opened his aunt's front gate at Number 17.

It was dark now, well after nine o'clock at night. Fred's Aunt Norah sat them down in the kitchen with cups of tea and bloater-paste sandwiches. Fred stayed up to play cribbage and drink a little whisky with his aunt, but the Bottle Rabbit, worn out by his day's town-adventures, soon went off to bed. As he lay curled up and warm he held on to his Magic Bottle and dreamt about a dark gold double-decker bus, full to the doors with kind white sheep and silent foreign white dachshunds. Pob, wearing a white top hat, was driving, and the conductress was an attractive young smiling white cat. When the bus stopped she put out a friendly paw and helped him on to it. The Bottle Rabbit smiled happily as he sank into the deepest sleep.